Anyone who's *anyone* digs

"Leslie Margolis's red-hot page-turn[...] first sentence. You won't be able to [...] until you reach the last sizzling wor[...]

—**Meg Cabot**, *New York Times* bestselling author
of The Princess Diaries series and *Pants on Fire*

"Smart, savvy, and with a refreshingly wicked streak, Jasmine Green is someone I could definitely hang out with. Thank you, Leslie Margolis, for writing us a character who is just as conflicted and imperfect as the rest of us. (Not that I am in any way suggesting that I am conflicted or imperfect. Because I'm totally not.)"

—**Samantha Bee**, senior correspondent for
The Daily Show with Jon Stewart

"With more twists than a bowl of fusilli and more sizzle than a pan of bacon, *Price of Admission* is the carbonara of novels: rich, salty, meaty—and impossible to resist."

—**E. Lockhart**, author of *The Boyfriend List* and
Fly on the Wall

"Forget the movies! For a great night of entertainment, pick up a tub of popcorn and this smart, funny, and outrageously scandalous novel."

—**Sarah Mlynowski**, author of the
Bras & Broomsticks trilogy

"Leslie Margolis's *Price of Admission* is naughty, noir, and lots of fun. And it definitely teaches you not to confuse life with the movies."

—**Maureen Johnson**, author of *13 Little Blue Envelopes*

"I can't remember the last time I discovered a heroine as achingly vulnerable and dead-on hilarious as Jasmine Green. Leslie Margolis's keen eye for Hollywood is utterly authentic—with all the attendant hypocrisy, humor, and tragedy—but Jasmine's voice is what gives the novel its rare and true soul."

—**Daniel Ehrenhaft**, Edgar Award–winning author
of *Drawing a Blank* and *The After Life*

Also by Leslie Margolis

Fix

More great reads from Simon Pulse

Confessions of a Backup Dancer

Reality Chick

Hazing Meri Sugarman

Meri Strikes Back

Dark Cindy

PRICE OF ADMISSION

LESLIE MARGOLIS

SIMON PULSE
New York | London | Toronto | Sydney

This book is a work of fiction. Any references to historical events, real people, or real locales are used fictitiously. Other names, characters, places, and incidents are the product of the author's imagination, and any resemblance to actual events or locales or persons, living or dead, is entirely coincidental.

SIMON PULSE
An imprint of Simon & Schuster Children's Publishing Division
1230 Avenue of the Americas, New York, NY 10020
Copyright © 2007 by Leslie Margolis
All rights reserved, including the right of reproduction in whole or in part in any form.
SIMON PULSE and colophon are registered trademarks of Simon & Schuster, Inc.
Designed by Steve Kennedy
The text of this book was set in Jante Antiqua.
Manufactured in the United States of America
First Simon Pulse edition February 2007
2 4 6 8 10 9 7 5 3 1
Library of Congress Control Number 2006928443
ISBN-13: 978-1-4169-2455-5
ISBN-10: 1-4169-2455-8

For Mitch. Yes, you.

Thank you Laura Langlie, Jennifer Klonsky, Bethany Buck,
Bill Contardi, Jessica Ziegler, Ethan Wolff,
Amanda McCormick, Julie Ann Hall,
Jim McGough, Mitchell Goldman,
Judy Goldman, and
Jim Margolis.

CHAPTER ONE

AUSTIN COOPER IS DEAD AND IT'S ALL MY FAULT.

That was the first thought that came to mind when Violet embraced me. My second was this: For someone so small and frail looking, her hug was intense. One of her bony shoulders dug into my neck, so it was hard to breathe. Caught by surprise, I wanted to shake her off, and only resisted because it would have looked bad. We were at Austin's memorial service. Practically everyone the Coopers knew was packed into this airless room. I didn't want to make things any worse.

Not that they could get much worse.

"It's still so hard, isn't it?" Violet gushed when she finally let go, her glassy eyes blinking.

"Hard" didn't cover my excruciating, soul-crushing agony.

It's been more than two months since Austin died, but I still feel as if it happened ten minutes ago. They found him on the sidewalk in front of Club Moomba, on Sunset Boulevard. He'd had a heart attack and died before the ambulance even made it to the hospital. I didn't sell him the Ecstasy or serve him the nine Red Bull and vodkas, or even strong-arm him into consuming so much toxic crap at once. To be honest, I wasn't even there when he OD'd. But I did see him earlier that night. Austin's time of death was 2:12 a.m., less than four hours after he'd left my place. He'd wanted to stay over, but I'd sent him away.

Since I couldn't admit this to anyone—especially not Violet, who'd been going out with Austin at the time—I didn't know what to say.

Turns out this didn't matter, because Violet kept right on talking. "A bunch of us are going to Chin Chin after the ceremony. It was Austin's favorite restaurant and—"

"I know what Austin's favorite restaurant was."

I didn't mean to snap, but I couldn't help it. Austin was my boyfriend first and I'd known him longer. Today would have been his twentieth birthday. I remember celebrating last year, when everything was good between us. Cruising down the Pacific Coast Highway with the top down and the music blaring. It was The Clash's "London Calling"—his choice but one of my favorites, too. At the beach we hung out on a deserted lifeguard station and watched the sun set over the Pacific. Austin had his guitar with him, and once it was dark, he played me a few of his new songs.

Back then he was too shy to perform in the light, even for an audience of one.

Back then he'd dedicated most of his songs to me.

Things changed, but none of that was Violet's fault. I wasn't even mad that she had started seeing Austin when he and I were—at least technically—still a couple. How can I be upset with her when I'm guilty of so much worse?

It's just, what I can't stop wondering about is how he could have been attracted to us both, when we could not be more different. Violet is tiny, with blond hair and blue eyes and when she's not grieving over her dead boyfriend, she's way too perky. She's the type of girl who bakes cupcakes topped with heart-shaped sprinkles, and makes her own greeting cards out of construction paper and glitter. Even though she's in college, her pens still bleed pink and purple ink. And me? Well, I'm everything that Violet is not, and a high school junior, to boot.

"So if you want to come with, you really should," Violet continued.

I hadn't even realized she was still talking.

Before I came up with an answer, someone else yelled, "Jasmine Green! There you are!"

Hearing my name, I turned around to find Lubna heading toward us. She's one of my best friends and ever since she left me here in L.A. to go to college up in Berkeley, I'd missed her like crazy.

Violet stepped back as Lubna swept in and gave me a hug— less bone-crushing and much needed.

"I'm so glad you're here," I cried, squeezing my eyes shut to keep my tears from falling.

"I wouldn't miss this," she said.

Letting go, she glared at Violet, who cowered. "Who are you?" Lubna asked.

Violet extended her hand warily. "I'm Violet," she said, as if that would explain everything.

Lubna ignored her hand and played dumb. "Violet?" she asked. "I don't think I've ever heard of you. How did you know Austin?" Even though Lubna moved here from Pakistan when she was seven, she still had a slight accent, which was cool because she could deliver insults in a way that made them sound like polite flattery.

I was used to it, but Violet seemed confused. "I'm, I mean, well, I was . . ." she paused, considering. "I was a friend of Austin's from UCLA. We lived in the same dorm."

"Oh," said Lubna, who knew exactly who Violet was.

"Well, I was just telling Jasmine that a bunch of us are going out to Chin Chin after the service," said Violet, bouncing back into cheerleader mode too quickly. "You guys should join us."

"Last time I went to Chin Chin I found a cockroach in my sesame chicken," Lubna said before turning her back on Violet.

As Violet headed back to her friends, I laughed. "That was subtle."

"Hey, it worked, didn't it?" Lubna smirked. "God, is she annoying. I can't believe she thinks she can just talk to you like nothing ever happened."

"I don't care about Violet," I said.

"She carries a Hello Kitty backpack, and not ironically," Lubna reminded me.

"When did you see a cockroach at Chin Chin?" I asked.

"Technically, never." Lubna flipped her long dark hair over one shoulder. "But it could happen."

"Maybe we should go," I said.

"You're kidding, right? Even if I wanted to, I couldn't. I'm leaving for London tonight and I still have to pack."

"Wait, you leave tonight?" I asked. "For how long?"

"I have to stay through New Year's and then I'm heading right back to school from there."

"So you'll be gone for all of Christmas vacation?" I asked, too surprised to care that I was talking loud enough to draw stares.

"Believe me, I'd much rather stay here than go to my cousin's wedding and see a million family members I don't even know, but I have no choice in the matter. I'm just glad I could make it today." Looking around, Lubna asked, "So where's your brother?"

"Don't know. I tried calling his cell, but you know Jett. . . ."

I didn't need to explain anything to Lubna. She'd dated my brother on and off back when they were in high school. She knew as well as I did that Jett lived in his own universe, where certain social norms—like the concept of time—just didn't apply and people loved him anyway. Grabbing my hand, she said, "Come on. Let's sit. It looks like the service is about to start."

There had to be more than two hundred people crammed into this too-small space, so Jett's lucky we were saving him a seat. Although "lucky" is a weird way to put it. No one ever hopes for great seats to their friend's memorial service.

It sucked to be here, and that was the biggest understatement of the day. The ceilings in this room were way too low and the lights too glaring. Some people talked in whispers, while others sat quietly, hands folded in their laps. No one knew how to act today. Everyone was so awkward—even Austin's former bandmates, Raven, T. J., and Scott, who were otherwise the epitome of cool.

All I wanted was for the service to start so that it would end and I could go home and forget all about the mess of the past six months. Put it behind me and try to get through Christmas vacation without completely losing my mind.

I trained my eyes on the door, itching to bolt, and that's when my brother cruised in. As soon as I saw him I stood up and waved. Jett is three years older than me, six feet tall and skinny. His coal-black hair hung messy over his forehead, not quite long enough to hide the piercing, dark intensity of his eyes. Even though he looked tired and troubled, practically every woman between the ages of fifteen and fifty was watching him. This was no surprise. As far back as I can remember, it's always been that way.

Looks-wise, Jett is a younger version of our dad. Both of them go through women like candy. Although so far only my dad has actually dated someone named Candy.

Personally, I don't see the attraction. But then again, I guess I'm not supposed to.

When Jett finally noticed us, he quickened his pace. "Hey, Lubna," he said, kissing her on the cheek.

"Where's Dad?" he asked after giving me a quick, one-armed hug. He smelled like the beach, and his hair was still damp from his post-surfing shower.

"He had a work thing," I said.

Jett grunted as he sat down next to me.

"The invite came last minute. He's going to that new director's house," I continued, feeling really bad, like it was somehow my fault. "Sophia Mancini is supposed to show, and he's trying to get her for his next movie, so he couldn't say no."

Jett was pissed, but he didn't say so. "As long as he has a good reason," he mumbled sarcastically. As if I were to blame for our dad's flakiness. Looking around, he asked, "How come we're sitting so far back?"

I shrugged. "I don't know. How close do you want to be?"

"Closer than this," Jett huffed.

Lubna leaned over me and poked Jett's knee, saying, "We're only back here because we were waiting for you outside. By the time we sat down, these were the only seats left."

There was another reason we weren't sitting closer, but I wasn't about to admit it. "I figured the front rows were reserved for family," I said instead.

"I've known Austin since kindergarten," Jett replied coldly. "That means we're family."

Lubna raised her eyebrows at me and I just shrugged.

My brother could be so self-righteous. Under any other circumstances it would be comical. He's the one who showed up late, so he had no right to complain. But it wasn't worth fighting about. Even if I'd wanted to, it was too late because Austin's dad was heading to the podium at the front of the room.

Dr. Cooper cleared his throat and said, "Hello and thank you all for being here to honor my son." His voice was slow and controlled, like he was struggling to hold back tears. Austin's dad is a strict, stodgy old Republican, and Austin couldn't stand him. But hearing him, just the tone of his voice, made me feel as if my whole body were caving inward.

Warm tears streamed down my face, but this time I didn't bother wiping them away. Hearing the sniffles of those around me, seeing so many squinty red eyes and crumpled tissues just made me cry harder.

Lubna grasped my hand, and even Jett put his arm around me.

I stared straight ahead. Dr. Cooper looked uncomfortable onstage, but then again, he was that type of guy—rigid and formal. He still made me call him Dr. Cooper even though his wife, who's also an MD, insists that I call her Lori. "As you all know, Austin was intelligent and sensitive," Dr. Cooper went on. "He planned to dedicate his life to helping others, which is why he was premed at UCLA. . . ."

Jett snorted and I elbowed him reflexively. Yes, we both knew that Austin was premed only because his parents had refused to pay for college otherwise, but this wasn't really the time. I shot him a look that said as much, but he just rolled his eyes and took his arm away.

Dr. Cooper went on. "Many of you have some thoughts to share, and a few of you will be performing songs, but before we begin, I have an announcement to make about an interesting new development. Is Marvin Green here?"

Jett glanced at me, confused. "What's this about?" he whispered.

I shrugged.

Everyone looked around in anticipation. Most of them recognized our dad's name, which was no surprise, because he's kind of famous. As the president and head of production of EggBrite Studios, Dad has been linked to a lot of big movies and even bigger movie stars, so he gets a ton of work-related press. He's not the only one, actually. People write about my whole family, and I'm not saying that to brag. It's just a fact and, to be honest, most of the time it sucks.

People *think* they know me because they've read about me or my parents or they've seen my picture in some magazine and they love me or hate me for it, usually without ever actually having spoken to me.

The most annoying part about it is, it's only because of our "tragic life circumstances" that certain reporters won't leave us alone. I was two and Jett was five when our mom, Marguerite, died. Twenty years ago, she was a famous actress.

Mom was also our dad's first wife, and according to the papers, he's "raised us by himself" ever since. Of course, the papers have a very loose interpretation of the word "raised," considering how little time our dad actually spends with us. Not that it's his fault. Marrying and divorcing six more wives over the course of fourteen years is time-consuming. (And I'm not even including his marriage from two summers ago, which technically ended in an annulment since Dad hadn't realized that his previous marriage wasn't yet legally terminated.)

Currently he's on wife number eight. GiGi Sinclair is a starlet, and they look cute together in pictures. My dad actually cares about that sort of thing a lot. He kind of has to, because in his business, image is everything. This may sound crazy, but I really think that having a scandalous, highly publicized love life makes him a more successful film executive. Like the young actresses he's paired with are just social currency, which he can convert into actual power. It's really messed up when you think about it too much, so I try not to.

That said, if the press knew what really went on at our house, they'd flip. It's the kind of thing that, if exposed, would make my dad the laughingstock of Hollywood. And who knows? It could even ruin his career.

"Marvin, would you like to come up here to say a few words?" Dr. Cooper asked.

Jett looked at me, and I knew what he was thinking: Dad hardly knew Austin. What was he going to say? And how was he going to say it when he wasn't even here?

Lubna leaned closer and whispered, "One of you needs to say something."

Clearly my brother was making no effort to handle this, so I jumped out of my seat and did my best to keep things short and to the point. "Um, Marvin—my dad, that is—he couldn't be here. He sends his regrets, though." I sat back down before Dr. Cooper could ask me any questions. No way was I about to admit that my dad was skipping the service for some stupid cocktail party.

Dr. Cooper seemed a bit taken aback, but seeing as how there was a huge crowd of people staring at him, he recovered quickly. "Okay, Jasmine. Thanks for letting us know. Well, then, I guess I'll have to make this announcement myself. I thought I knew everything about my son—a great athlete, who dreamed of becoming a doctor. But I didn't know that he was a writer, too. It wasn't until my wife and I were cleaning out Austin's dorm room at UCLA a few weeks ago that we learned he was working on a screenplay. We read it and were shocked, because even though it was unfinished, it was obviously something great. We sent it to our friend, who's an agent, and she sent it to the film studios, and to make a long story short, Austin's screenplay, *Cold-Blooded, Two-Timing Rat*, was just optioned by Marvin Green, the president and head of production at EggBrite Studios. Austin's work is going to be turned into a movie."

Piercing sirens went off in the room. That's what I thought, anyway. It took a few moments to realize that the noise was all in my head. Dr. Cooper was still talking—or at least his lips were moving—but I couldn't hear a thing. Nor could I move since my entire body felt numb. I was shocked, amazed, dumbfounded, and, most of all, utterly horrified.

This couldn't actually be happening. It had to be some sort of cruel and twisted joke.

Jett leaned over and whispered something in my ear.

"What?" I asked, not hearing a thing.

"Did you know anything about this?" he asked.

I tried to swallow the lump that was forming in my throat, but it kept on growing. Not that it mattered, because even if I'd wanted to, I couldn't answer Jett. Not honestly, anyway. I was too busy freaking out, because Austin wasn't a writer. Or at least, he didn't write *Cold-Blooded, Two-Timing Rat.*

I did. And it's not just a screenplay. It's the story of my life.

CHAPTER TWO

COLD-BLOODED, TWO-TIMING RAT

Opening scene:

The phone is ringing as the camera pans the bedroom of seventeen-year-old Jessica Brown. She's asleep in a large room. She's wearing a big T-shirt, and the blankets are pushed to one side. Next to her, under the covers, is a guy, but just his blond hair and part of his face are visible.

Early morning sun streams in through the window. Clothes are strewn on the polished wood floor. Indie rock posters adorn the walls: Bright Eyes, Björk, Modest Mouse, Wilco, Clap Your Hands Say Yeah, etc.

On the sixth ring she picks up.

                    JESS (sleepily)
        What?

Voice of (V.O.) BARRY WENTWORTH, *Starlife* magazine reporter

               BARRY
   So what do you think about your
   father's latest marriage?

Jess sits up with a start.

               JESS
   Barry. I thought we had a deal.

               BARRY
   No calls before nine a.m. on the
   weekends, yeah, yeah, I remember.
   But this is an emergency.

Jess rubs her eyes.

               JESS
   What emergency? Off the record, my
   dad gets married all the time. That
   was OFF RECORD. It shows up, I'm
   calling your boss. No, I'm having our
   lawyer call your boss.

               BARRY
   I don't need a sixteen-year-old
   telling me how to do my job. I know
   what off the record means.

Jess lifts up the wrist of the sleeping guy next to
her and glances at his watch. When she lets go, it
lands with a thud but the guy doesn't stir.

               JESS
   It's not even eight o'clock. And I'm

seventeen now, remember? Wasn't it
you who crashed my birthday party
last year and took pictures, which
you later sold to *Teen People*? I told
you how much flak I got for that at
school the next day. And what did you
promise me then? "No gratuitous
calls," wasn't it?

                    BARRY
Give a guy a break. We've all gotta
eat. Not everyone was born into
Hollywood royalty like you. Some
people have to work for a living.

                    JESS
Dude, stop trying to make me feel
sorry for you. I've seen your car.
Starving reporters don't drive BMWs.

                    BARRY
It's leased. And my next payment is
due. So, about the new marriage . . .

Off shot (O.S.) Jake, Jess's older brother,
screaming from downstairs.

                  O.S. JAKE
JESS! JESSICA! ARE YOU UP? JESSICA,
YOU'RE NOT GOING TO FUCKING BELIEVE
THIS.

The guy in bed with Jess turns over, groans, and
places a pillow over his head. She shushes him.

                    BARRY
What's going on there? Sounds like
someone isn't taking the news so well.

                    JESS
I've gotta go.

                    BARRY
The quote?

                    JESS
Um, We're thrilled for Dad and
excited to welcome his new wife into
the family.

Jess clicks the phone off and throws it on her bed,
then bolts out of the room, downstairs to
the kitchen.

Hunched over the paper at the kitchen counter is
her brother, Jake. Tall, thin. Same dark hair and
same green eyes as Jess.

                    JESS
    What?

Jake holds up the front page of the L.A. Times.
Camera zooms in on headline: LAS VEGAS WEDDING
BELLS FOR STUDIO CHIEF MAX BROWN AND HIS LEAD ACTRESS,
GINGER BELL.

                    JAKE
Fucking Dad got married, again.

Jess grabs the paper. Reads the story. Looks up at Jake and opens her mouth to talk, but no words come out. She stares down at the paper, again, in utter disbelief.

> JESS
> Ginger Bell? Isn't she, like, nineteen?

> JAKE
> She's twenty-three. Three years older than me. We could have gone to high school together.

Jess reads the article.

> JESS
> Except she went to high school in Pleasant Valley, Nebraska. Where the hell is that, anyway? It sounds like a cult, not a town.

> JAKE
> This sucks. He said he'd wait awhile, after the last mess. Fuck. I am *not* living with this. I'm moving out. Really, I am.

> JESS
> You've been saying that for two years.

Phone rings again. Jake backs away from it and throws up his hands.

                              JAKE
                 I can't deal with this now.

                              JESS
                 I got the last call. Barry woke me up.

Jake picks up the phone and shouts into it.

                              JAKE
                 Fuck you, we have no comment, and
                 don't call here anymore.

Jake looks confused.

                              JAKE
                 Oh hi, Chad. Sorry about that.

Jake hands Jess the phone.

                              JAKE
                 Why is your math tutor calling you
                 this early on a Sunday?

Shocked, Jess grabs the phone and runs back upstairs.

                              JESS
                 Chad? What's up?

                              CHAD
                 Alex is here.

Jess bursts into her bedroom. We see Chad on his cell
phone. He's tall, thin, nerdy-cute, and totally
panicked.

Chad drops the phone and continues getting
dressed, frantically. His hair is a mess. His
T-shirt is on inside out. He's fumbling with the
zipper on his jeans.

Jess runs to the window facing the street and sees
Alex walking up to the front door.

> JESS
> What's he doing here?

> CHAD
> Don't know. He's your boyfriend.

> JESS
> I'm so sorry. This is so screwed up.

Jess tries to kiss Chad, but he backs away.

> CHAD
> This is bullshit, Jess. You've got to
> break up with him.

> JESS
> You know it's not that simple.

> CHAD
> If you don't tell him soon, I will.

> JESS
> You don't mean that.

                        CHAD
            Yeah, this time I really do. I swear.

He heads out the window facing the side of the
house, climbs over the balcony, and scrambles
down the trellis. On his jump down, he twists his
ankle and yelps.

Jess cringes.

Chad runs/limps away without looking back.

Jess goes back downstairs and opens up the front
door. Alex is standing there—tall, broad-shouldered,
with long dark hair and small round glasses. He's
wearing ripped jeans and an old Pixies concert
T-shirt.

                        JESS
        Hey.

                        ALEX
        Hi.

They kiss.

                        ALEX
            Why are you so out of breath?

                        JESS
            What are you doing here?

ALEX

I was up early and I saw the news
about your dad.

JESS

It was on the news?

ALEX

It was the top story on the E! channel.
So, are you okay?

JESS

I'm fine. I mean, you know, I'll be
fine. My dad does this all the time.
I should be used to it by now.

ALEX

Well, since we're both up, do you
want to get some breakfast? I still
have an hour to kill before I can
pick up my tux.

JESS

Your tux?

ALEX

For my parents' anniversary party
tonight, remember? You're still
coming with me, aren't you?

JESS

Uh, sure. Of course.

Alex hugs Jessica.

                    ALEX
         Don't worry, babe. I'm here for you.
         Everything's going to be okay.

Close-up of Jess's face, which reads equal parts
guilt, horror, and relief.

CHAPTER THREE

THE FIRST SCENES I'D MEMORIZED, AND AS I SPED home I replayed them in my head. Anyone who read the script—even just up to that point—would totally recognize me, and would therefore know that I'm a two-timing rat. Cheating on my boyfriend, who was sweet and caring and sensitive enough to be concerned about my emotional well-being in the face of my father's eighth marriage? It was horrible. I'm horrible, and now everyone is going to know. Still, that's nothing compared to what I wrote about later. . . .

If only I'd disguised my life better. I mean, I could have done more than change everyone's name. And even that is so obvious when you think about it for half a second. The lead character, Jessica Brown, has green eyes, and I, Jasmine Green, have brown eyes. That's the only difference between us. Same with my brother, Jett/Jake.

Charlie and Austin? Sure, I call them Chad and Alex, but they're so clearly the same people. Anyone who reads this and knows them will definitely recognize their personalities. I did nothing to disguise their looks, either, with the exception of giving Austin Charlie's glasses. (I figured it was too cliché to give the athletic musician perfect vision while making the sci-fi–loving computer geek suffer from severe near-sightedness, even though that's actually the case in real life.)

But they're not even the ones I care about the most. It's all the stuff about GiGi and Jett that really stresses me out.

My dad must know the truth by now. So, what was he thinking, buying the rights? How has he not had a heart attack? Is it because he's plotting to kill me? And GiGi and Jett, for that matter? Me, my stepmom, and my brother—no one is innocent in this. We've all betrayed him in our own way.

As I turned off Laurel Canyon onto our steep and windy driveway, my heart started beating faster. Normally, getting closer to home relaxes me. We have lots of trees all over our property and our house is up on a hill and by the time you get there, you can forget that you're living in a smoggy city and some jerk just honked at you for taking too long to go at a green light because you were busy trying to find a different playlist on your iPod. Today the sight of home did nothing to calm my nerves. This was a bad sign.

I love our house. It's a Mediterranean-style villa with a red-tiled roof. The beige stucco sides are half covered in ivy, and there are pretty blue shutters on every window with matching window boxes filled with colorful flowers. The house is big but not so big that it feels like a museum or anything. Even when it's occupied by one of Dad's soon-to-be-ex-wives, there's still plenty of space to get away and relax.

My mom lived here on her own, before she met my dad, and I know from her old interviews that she saw the place as "a hidden oasis of tranquility and calm in the never-ending storm that is Hollywood." Ever since reading that, it's been hard for me not to agree, especially since the house is almost the same as it was when my parents lived there together. Sure, now there's an extra wing out back, courtesy of Minnie Le Rue, wife number four, but she was out of the picture before the construction crew even broke ground.

As I parked I noticed that Dad's car was in the driveway. His car-detailer, Raj, was outside waxing it, which was encouraging. As I waved I realized that my dad isn't stupid. If he were going to murder our entire household he'd certainly make sure there weren't any witnesses around.

And the rest of the grounds were crowded as usual. Juan, the new landscape architect, was just leaving, but not rushing away like he'd been told to scram. He and his three assistants were totally taking their time, carefully placing all the old rosebushes into large black garbage bags. (Last week, GiGi had insisted that the red ones be replaced with pink ones, and no one else cared enough to disagree.)

The pool guy's old blue pickup was parked at the curb. Well, one tire was actually on the curb, which was typical. His back window is so heavily plastered with old Phish decals, he can't see out of it. That meant Joe was out back cleaning the pool, where there are views into our house from practically every angle. Joe would definitely be able to see everything if Dad tried to kill me, and he could so easily turn the pool skimmer into a weapon of defense.

The black skirt I'd worn to Austin's service was hot and itchy and my heels were giving me serious blisters, but I didn't bother changing. That would have taken too much time, and I had to know what was going on. As soon as I walked inside, I headed to my dad's office, where he spent most of his time when he wasn't sleeping or at his real office, in Beverly Hills. He was on the phone but told me he'd be just be a minute.

Falling into the chair opposite his desk, I slipped off my shoes and waited. And waited and waited. The longer I sat there, the worse I felt.

Dad always seems so sure of himself and happy when he's working. Seeing him there, laughing into the phone, sitting in front of his huge bookcase, which didn't actually contain any books—just shiny, gold Oscar statuettes and framed pictures of himself with various celebrities—all made me feel so guilty. He's a really great guy, in so many ways.

Right after Mom died, her sister, Peggy, offered to raise us. Since Dad works 24/7, she figured anyone in his position would see two young kids as burdens. But she lives in Northern California, in this tiny town just a few miles away from the Oregon border. Dad said no way was he going to give us up when we were all that he had. He hired round-the-clock nannies, spent what little time with us he could, and the issue never came up again.

Now that we're pretty much grown (although sometimes I wonder about Jett), we obviously don't need babysitters anymore, but Dad is still as hands-on as he can be. Regardless of whom he's marrying, he always makes sure his new wives know that Jett and I come first. (Or at least second, after his job, but who can blame him for that? He has a very important job.)

And about all those wives. I'm not stupid. I know that obviously most women are attracted to Dad because he's successful and can get them great parts in blockbuster movies and he's got a lot of money and whatever, but besides all that extra stuff, he's actually cute and sweet, too. You know, for an old guy. He's tall, with longish dark hair and big brown eyes, like Jett, but without the brooding angst. He dresses well, in simple dark suits with clean T-shirts and sneakers, and he's fairly hip. I guess it's part of his job and everything, but it's still cool that my dad can see beyond Eminem's raunchy lyrics to understand and embrace his true musical genius.

I didn't mean to make him sound so oblivious and uncaring

in my screenplay. I just wrote what I saw, and somehow he ended up sounding like a pathetic and somewhat callous jerk.

At the same time, for all those pictures behind him—Dad with Kate Hudson, Dad with Angelina Jolie, Dad with Gwen Stefani and Beyoncé, and Dad with the cast of *Desperate Housewives*—there wasn't one shot of Dad with Jett and me. Not that I'd ever say anything to him about it, but it would have been nice if he'd decided to put one up on his own. Even if it was just a small one.

As I waited, I started to notice that my dad didn't seem angry or even upset, which was weird. I mean, I wrote a screenplay that exposed our family's worst secrets. Secrets he hadn't even known about. And once everyone found out the truth, we'd all be humiliated—Dad most of all.

Yet here he was on the phone, calmly negotiating with some crazy movie star who wanted to use the company jet for a Scientology retreat in Wyoming.

"If it were up to me, Ted, I'd let you take it in a second," my dad said. "But we're a publicly traded company, and the board wouldn't be happy."

Dad winked at me. He seemed so calm. How could that be? Unless . . .

Suddenly it hit me. My dad must be so relaxed because he's already taken care of the situation. Here's what must have happened: Dad read the script, recognized all of the characters, and then bought it so he could bury the story by keeping the movie from ever getting made. You see, even though EggBrite Studios puts out about twenty-five movies a year, for every six stories they buy in-house, only one actually makes it through development to production, to postproduction, and then to release. One in six, while the rest get stuck somewhere along the way and end up in a state of permanent limbo.

There are writers (very bitter writers) who thought they'd hit the jackpot when their screenplays were bought ten years ago only to find out that *selling* their movie scripts didn't necessarily translate into their work *becoming* actual movies on the big screen.

This made me feel better, because obviously I never intended for the screenplay to be sold. It was my diary, in screenplay format.

It was a huge relief to know that none of us would be publicly humiliated. Clearly my dad bought the story before too many other people read it. All those scandalous details would never get leaked to the press, and his image would remain intact. Moreover, he would dump GiGi, she'd move back to Nebraska or Tarzana or wherever, and the rest of us could get on with our lives.

Although this still meant that I had a lot of explaining to do. I just didn't know where to begin.

When he finally hung up and said, "So, about this Austin thing . . . ," I braced myself. Here it comes. Is he going to disown me? Throw me out? Ask me for the keys to my Mustang? (I hope not. I love that car. It's a black convertible, circa 1968. Dad got it for me when I turned sixteen. Okay, actually, he got it for me a month later, out of guilt for having to be at the Cannes Film Festival in France on my actual birthday, but that doesn't matter. It's a really, really cool car.)

He crossed his arms over his chest and leaned back. "I'm sorry about missing the service."

"You should have been there," I said.

"No kidding. I heard about Ron Cooper's announcement. He wasn't supposed to say anything until it was a done deal."

Okay, my dad was so missing the point. But wait a second. "You mean it's not?" I asked.

"We definitely want to buy the script, but we're still negotiating the terms and nothing has been signed. For someone who claims to be doing this all in the name of his late son's memory, Ron is getting very greedy. He obviously made the announcement in front of the large crowd to try to put pressure on the studio."

"That's so sleazy. Austin would've hated that." Okay, I know I was supposed to be worried about my dad's feelings and this enormous secret that was going to ruin his life, but hearing about Dr. Cooper made my skin crawl. I mean, it's not even his work. It's not even the work of anyone he's related to.

This would be a great time to confess. All I had to do was say the words: *It's mine.* Put an end to all this. That would be the safe, smart thing to do, right? Confess and then take the flak that I surely deserved. And I was going to do it. Really, I was. But before I did, I had to ask, "So you liked it?"

Dad nodded. "Of course. It's great."

"Really?" I half expected my dad to say, "Yes, and I hope it was worth it because you have exactly thirty minutes to pack your things and leave this house."

Although he can't legally do that, since I'm still a minor for another five months.

"Well, I'm told it's great," my dad continued. "I haven't had a chance to look at it yet, but it's gotten great coverage."

I can't believe this didn't occur to me before. Coverage, for a movie business executive, is what SparkNotes are to any high school student with a term paper due at the end of the week. But actually coverage is better than SparkNotes, because coverage is usually only one page long. Plus, it's the "real world," so rather than getting penalized for having others do their work, Hollywood executives are paid copious amounts of money for it.

The thing is, if a screenplay gets really great coverage, it can get bought and go into production without certain higher-ups ever reading a word. This meant that my dad had no idea what his company was about to buy. At some point he'd learn, but by then it might be too late.

Of course, this also meant that people liked my work. Strangers and professionals, not just teachers whose job it is to encourage me. "Um, can I see it?" I asked. "The coverage."

"Of course." My dad handed me a stack of pages.

Cold-Blooded, Two-Timing Rat, by Austin Cooper, is a story of deception, heartbreak, love, lust, and the ultimate betrayal. It's told from the P. O. V. of Jessica Brown, the daughter of a Hollywood player, and set against a glamorous backdrop of glistening swimming pools, clear blue skies, fancy cars, beautiful people, and fabulous parties. Fresh, complex, unique, and hilarious but with a heart, this is sure to be a hit. Think *Clueless* meets *The Graduate*, but centered around a rich, hot, teenage Lisa Simpson.

* Considering the young age and dramatic death of the author, the marketing possibilities are endless.

Flipping through the rest of it, I saw the words "brilliant," "titillating," "witty," and "shockingly authentic." Some people compared my story to the movie *Less Than Zero.* Others said it was the next *American Pie,* which, as long as they were talking about the first one, was pretty flattering. Every single page mentioned Austin's age and his dramatic death. I was stunned and speechless.

"Who knew Austin had it in him," Dad said, to which I could only cough. Luckily, he didn't seem to notice. Leaning back in his chair, he continued: "It's rare to see so much positive coverage across the board. I've seen a lot of scripts about Hollywood and quite frankly, most of them miss the mark, focusing on the clichés rather than authentic characters. Apparently, this one's really got something. It makes sense, of course. Even though Austin's parents are doctors, he spent so much time around here with you and Jett. It's understandable that he'd pick up a lot of the milieu."

I grunted. It wasn't brilliant, but it was all I could manage to get out at the moment. My life was on the verge of becoming a horrible train wreck. This screenplay would destroy my father and our whole family and he had no idea. I had to put a stop to this, now. But that would mean telling my dad the truth. Where was I supposed to begin? I couldn't just blurt it out.

Um, Dad . . . Jett and GiGi are having an affair. Yes, you heard me right. Your wife and your son have been sneaking around behind your back. I've known about it for months, and I never said a word to you. Instead, I wrote about it in my diary, which looks like a screenplay. And then I gave it to Austin, because, well, because it's complicated, and that's beside the point.

No. There was no way. I couldn't tell my dad that I'd turned this private family catastrophe into some sordid story that will probably end up on *Access Hollywood*.

His ego couldn't take it. And what would happen to Jett? No way would Dad forgive him. So would he kick both of us out? Jett could not survive on the streets of Beverly Hills, on his own. Jett could not even survive in college. We moved him into his USC dorm room a year and a half ago. He came back the next day, claiming he couldn't figure out how to hang his plasma-screen TV on the dorm's cinderblock walls. He hasn't spent a night on campus since.

This was beyond terrible.

"Are you okay, Jazzy?" asked my dad.

"Fine." I gulped. "I mean, great. I mean, well, I just feel bad for Austin. That he's missing all this. I just, I really wish he was here right now." It was hard, but I handed the stack of coverage back to my dad. He didn't even notice that my hands were shaking.

"I know this must be hard for you. . . ."

The way he stared at me, it made me wonder. Did he really know? Was he trying to trick me into telling him the truth? If that was the case, what was I waiting for?

I opened my mouth to apologize, already feeling the tears creeping into my eyes. But before I managed to say a word, he sighed and said, "So much death at such a young age."

Oh, right, that. I hate it when people bring up the fact that my mom died when I was so young. As if that explains every-thing about me. The truth is, I remember very little about her, which also makes me feel crappy. Of course I wish that things were different, but they're not. I don't want anyone feeling sorry for me, ever, especially not my dad, who should know better.

I didn't know how to respond. I never do when she comes up. It didn't matter, anyway, because the phone was ringing, and Dad frowned at his caller ID and picked it up, saying, by way of an apology, I guess, "I have to take this."

I wanted to leave but couldn't. There was still time to con-fess. If only I could figure out how.

When my dad finally noticed I was still frozen in my seat, he cupped his hand over the mouthpiece of the phone.

"Do me a favor, Jazzy?" he whispered, pulling a screenplay from the middle of his stack and tossing it to me. "Will you read it and let me know what you think? You have time, right? I'd do it myself, but I'm completely swamped here."

"Okay," I whispered.

"Unless you're too busy with school and everything."

"It's winter break," I reminded him. I'm surprised he forgot, since he had a big movie coming out on Christmas Day, which was this Friday.

On the other hand, school stuff wasn't exactly on his radar. Whenever a star from one of his movies was going to be interviewed on *Letterman* or *The Daily Show*, he encouraged me to stay up late and watch. Telling him I needed my sleep because I had a big test the next morning was never a valid excuse. Nor was offering to watch it on TiVo the following day. No, I had to be there in the moment, to witness his moment of glory. And, okay, I must admit—it's fun seeing him so happy. Movies were what mattered to him the most. If I wanted to have anything in common with him, to relate to him in any way, I had to care too. Or at least I had to pretend to.

"So you'll read it?" he asked.

"Sure," I replied, trying to force some enthusiasm. "I'd love to."

"Great. Try to finish it in the next few days, will you? I'll take you out for dim sum and you can tell me all about it."

"Perfect," I said, even though I hate dim sum. Regular Chinese food is fine, but dim sum is too greasy and it gives me a headache. I've told my dad this on numerous occasions, but he never remembers. Not that it mattered, since there were bigger things to worry about.

I stared at the so-called screenplay with this weird mix of dread and curiosity. I'd only ever printed out one copy—the one I'd given to Austin, unsigned. I wondered how many were out there now.

CHAPTER FOUR

Jess pulls up to the Hotel Bel-Air in her 1968 red Mustang convertible. She leaves her car with the valet, gives her name at the door, walks past security guards, and enters the party.

The camera pans the room. The scene is elegant but over the top—all tuxedos and ball gowns.

Jess wears a funky sage green dress with matching platform heels. She walks past a champagne fountain, a chocolate fountain, and finally an ice sculpture of a boy peeing vodka.

Jess sees Chad and starts to approach. They haven't spoken since he fled her room that morning. She desperately wants to be with him, but he shakes his head no. She stops in her tracks. Just then her boyfriend, Alex, comes over from the other direction, wraps his arms around her, and kisses her hello.

                    ALEX
Hey.

                    JESS
Hey, yourself.

                    ALEX
You're late.

                    JESS
I know, but I look fabulous. It takes
time.

                    ALEX
What do you want to drink?

                    JESS
Just a Coke.

                    ALEX
High school chicks.

Jess takes Alex's arm as they walk toward the bar.
She notices that he's unsteady on his feet.

                    JESS
How many drinks have you had tonight?

                    ALEX
Not enough to dull the pain.

                    JESS
It's only eight o'clock, Alex. How
much pain can you be in?

                        ALEX
You have no idea.

                        JESS
You should slow down.

                        ALEX
But I'm celebrating. Think about it,
babe. How often do my parents have an
anniversary?

                        JESS
a) Don't call me babe. And b) If you
need me to answer that question, you've
definitely had too much to drink.

Alex turns to the bartender and orders Jess
a soda and himself a double scotch on the rocks.
Jess frowns at him, disapproving. He ignores her.
On the way back from the bar they run into Loretta
Davies—Alex's mom, a tall, elegant, older woman.
She and Jess air kiss.

                        ALEX
Hi, Mom.

                        JESS
Happy anniversary, Loretta.

                        LORETTA
Thanks, dear. You look lovely.

                         MAX
        As do you.

Max comes over and surprises Jess. He's tall and
distinguished looking with short, salt-and-pepper
hair.

Jess is visibly annoyed.

                         JESS
        What are you doing here?

                         MAX
        I was invited. Nice way to talk to your
        father.

                         JESS
        Sorry. I thought you were still in
        Vegas.

                         MAX
        We had to get back. Ginger is reading
        for a part tomorrow morning.

                         JESS
        You mean she's here? You actually
        brought her here?

                         MAX
        Of course I brought her. She's my wife.

                         JESS
        Yes, but only since five minutes ago.

Max ignores Jess and turns to Loretta.

                          MAX
          Happy anniversary, Loretta. How many
          years has it been?

                        LORETTA
          Twenty-five years of marriage, if you
          don't count the two-year separation.

                          MAX
          Very impressive.

Jess rolls her eyes and mutters something
sarcastic to Alex. He isn't paying attention. No
one is, because everyone is watching Ginger
approach.

Ginger is tall and beautiful, with long, silky
black hair, deeply tanned skin, and blue eyes.
She's dressed in a slinky white dress, and her
boobs are pouring out over the top. They are
obviously fake.

This doesn't stop Alex from gawking. Jess notices
and is annoyed.

Ginger comes closer, kisses Max on the cheek, and
links her arm in his. Her voice is a babyish
squeak.

                        GINGER
          There you are.

MAX
Ginger, meet my daughter, Jess.

Much to Jess's surprise, Ginger squeals and
embraces her.

GINGER
I've heard so much about you. It's
wonderful to finally meet you.

Jess is annoyed by all the phoniness but tries to
hide it. She backs away.

JESS
Um, you too.

MAX
And this is Loretta Davies.

Ginger and Loretta air-kiss.

GINGER
Fabulous party.

Alex coughs. He can't keep his eyes off Ginger's
cleavage. Jess is seething.

LORETTA
Thank you, dear. Have you met my oldest
son, Alex?

Alex kisses her on the cheek.

                         Alex
I'm Jess's boyfriend, so, uh, we'll be
seeing a lot of each other. By the way,
I'm a big fan. You were so kick-ass in
Death Slayer, Part Three.

                        GINGER
Thank you so much. That was a silly
movie, though. I hope to branch out
into more serious work.

     JESS (STARING POINTEDLY AT HER FATHER)
I'll bet you do.

Max shrugs, as if to say, "What do you expect?"

Ginger doesn't notice. She continues talking to
Alex.

                        GINGER
You look very familiar. Are you an
actor?

Alex pretends to be bashful but is obviously
enjoying the moment.

                         ALEX
No, but I play guitar for the band
Canadian Bacon. Maybe you saw us at the
Roxy last week.

                         MAX
Impossible. Ginger is a strict
vegetarian.

Everyone laughs at the corny joke, just to be polite.
Everyone but Ginger, that is. She seems confused.

> GINGER (TO MAX)
> I'm not a vegetarian. I'm just trying
> to go macrobiotic.

> MAX
> Of course you are, dear.

Awkward pause. Then Ginger turns to Alex.

> GINGER
> I don't think I've heard of you.

> ALEX
> You should come see us sometime.

> GINGER
> Well, at the very least I'll buy your
> CDs.

> ALEX
> Um, we don't have any yet. We're
> working on a demo, though.

> LORETTA
> Alex is premed at UCLA.

> GINGER
> That's wonderful. Education is so
> important. That's why I didn't even
> think about coming to Los Angeles
> until I got my GDP.

                              JESS
    You mean your GED?

                             GINGER
    Isn't that what I said?

Suddenly Chad approaches. He trips over a small
step, stumbles, and spills an entire glass of red
wine down the front of Ginger's white dress.
Ginger screams.

                              CHAD
        Oh, no. I don't know how that happened.
        I'm so sorry. I can't believe I'm such
        a klutz.

As everyone fumbles with napkins for Ginger, Chad
winks at Jess. She realizes he doused her in wine on
purpose, for her, and smiles.

Loretta is annoyed and embarrassed.

                            LORETTA
        I'm so sorry, Ginger. This is my other
        son, Chad. He should really come with a
        warning label.

CHAPTER FIVE

Dirty little secret number two, revealed in just the first few scenes: I was cheating on Austin with his younger brother, Charlie, although it's not as bad as it sounds. Yes, it was sleazy and cold-hearted, but Austin and I had been growing apart for a while, and he was cheating on me, too, with Violet. Not that this makes it right. I'm just saying, we were going to break up anyway.

It must seem weird—writing about myself in such an unflattering way, but when I started the screenplay, I never thought anyone would actually read it. I was just so confused and fed up and angry and I had no one to talk to about it.

Writing was my only safe way of venting.

If Carmen hadn't left, none of this ever would have happened. I know it seems crazy, blaming this all on my nanny when I'm seventeen years old, but Carmen was so much more than that. She lived with us and took care of me and Jett for eleven years. As we grew up, her role morphed from nanny into older sister/surrogate mom/best friend and my all-around favorite person in the world. She also ran our entire household, hounded me and Jett to do our homework, and convinced my dad that certain girlfriends were wholly inappropriate and had to be dropped, immediately.

If Carmen hadn't moved out last year, GiGi never would have survived at our house, and she never would have gotten away with what she did.

Not that I thought Carmen would live with us forever. That wouldn't be fair. She had her own life too. She'd just finished business school and was working at some big venture capital firm and had this great apartment in Santa Monica. I was happy things were going so well for her. Yet a big part of me wished she was still around, especially now, when everything was falling apart.

I dialed Carmen's number, thinking maybe she'd want to go to yoga with me tomorrow. We'd go out for chai lattes after, and eventually I'd confess and she'd come up with some brilliant solution that would make everything right again. It wasn't until I got her machine that I remembered her little sister in El Salvador was about to have twins and Carmen was staying with her for two whole weeks. Apparently her phone wasn't working down there.

As I hung up I heard GiGi's voice over the intercom. "Dinner's ready," she called.

I hid the screenplay under my bed—as if there weren't at least fifty copies circulating around town—and headed downstairs. We all piled into Dad's Jaguar and drove down the hill to Sushi Yuki on Sunset Boulevard.

We've been going to Sushi Yuki every Sunday night since Dad's third marriage to Marla, a therapist, who was convinced that Jett and I needed more stability in our lives. Her solution was a consistent weekly dinner. Marla ended up leaving Dad for her Pilates instructor, a few months after bestowing us with this wisdom, but we like the Sunday night family thing, so we've kept it up.

As usual, our corner table was ready when we got to the

restaurant. Sanjay the DJ was spinning at the other end of the room. The place was packed with a scantily dressed crowd, which I didn't quite get, since the air-conditioning was blasting. I was wearing my favorite tan suede jacket over a white tank top with dark blue jeans, and I still had goose bumps.

The second we sat down, our waitress, Sheryl, brought us a large bowl of edamame and a pitcher of passion fruit iced tea. "You want the usual?" she asked.

"Yeah, but I'll have an extra-spicy tuna roll and two more pieces of unagi, please," said Jett. "I'm starving."

"I'm not that hungry," said GiGi. "I'll go straight to the sashimi."

GiGi always went straight to the sashimi. According to her, eating white rice is one of the seven deadly sins. I think she ranked it just above wearing last year's Manolo Blahniks. Too bad that "cheating on your husband with his son" didn't even make her list.

After everyone ordered, Dad said, "I think I can manage to get away from the office for a few days. How would you guys feel about taking a quick ski trip next week? We can leave on Christmas morning."

"I'd rather go to Hawaii," said Jett.

"Ooh, Hawaii," GiGi cooed as she poured iced tea for the table.

"I can't be that far away with the new Henkly brothers picture coming out," said Dad. "I was thinking Colorado. Aspen or Telluride? Which do you prefer?"

"Hawaii," said GiGi. "I was only there once, to do a Noxema commercial, but I really loved it and I've been wanting to get back there ever since."

Poor Dad. He tries so hard and he has no idea how awful we all are.

"We haven't been to Colorado in ages," I pointed out. "I'd

love to go skiing." Even if this weren't true I would have said it. I hate it when GiGi and Jett gang up on Dad. These days it's happening more and more.

"Last time I went skiing I tore my ACL," said GiGi. "And while it was great that I lost a lot of weight after the surgery, I really can't take that risk now. If I break a bone, I won't be able to work for weeks."

"She has a point, Dad," said Jett. "You're not the only one with a career to think about."

GiGi raised her sunglasses and surveyed the room. Yes, GiGi was wearing sunglasses inside. And, yes, she was wearing them so she wouldn't be recognized and, yes, she was now panning the restaurant to see if *she* recognized anyone. The worst part was that with Carmen gone and Jett so enamored with GiGi, I had no one to point out this hypocrisy to.

Suddenly GiGi gasped. "Is that Justin Riley?" she asked, pointing toward the farthest corner of the restaurant.

"You've got to be kidding me," I muttered under my breath. If anyone heard me, they didn't let on.

Dad glanced over his shoulder. "Looks like it," he said.

"Do you know him?" GiGi grabbed my dad's arm, clinging to him as if she were about to be swept away in a strong ocean current. Although, perhaps that's just wishful thinking on my part.

"Of course." My dad seemed insulted. "We go way back. He was in *Mighty Little Giants* in 2004."

"Well, everyone's expecting great things from his directorial debut. And he's still casting, so will you introduce me?" asked GiGi. "My agent has been trying to get me an audition with him for weeks." Her sunglasses were now propped on top of her head. So excited to meet him, she was practically foaming at the mouth.

Meanwhile, Justin Riley was eating sushi with his fingers at the other end of the restaurant. He was sandwiched between two women, who wore matching too-tight halter tops, probably on purpose so they could call attention to their monster-size fake boobs.

I looked to Jett, who stared down at his empty plate, embarrassed. At least he still had enough sense to know when GiGi was acting ridiculous.

Somehow Dad managed to keep a straight face. All the while, I could read the annoyance in his eyes. He folded his napkin and stood up, saying, "Come on, GiGi. I'll introduce you. You kids want to come?"

"No," we both said at the same time.

And then they were off.

I don't know how my dad put up with it. There's nothing less cool than going up to a celebrity when he or she's trying to eat dinner in peace. I guess no one ever recognized GiGi and interrupted her meals, because if anyone did, she'd know better. Not that I could point this out to my brother, who was one of her biggest fans.

Left alone, Jett and I didn't have much to say to each other. I watched him drum his chopsticks against the side of the table. It used to be that "dressy" for my brother meant wearing tennis shoes instead of flip-flops, but then GiGi came along. Tonight he was wearing a long-sleeved black shirt tucked into khakis. Even worse, he was wearing a pair of chocolate-brown leather man-sandals. Jett used to make fun of guys who wore man-sandals. For good reason.

Come to think of it, those looked like women's sandals.

"Where did you get those?" I asked.

Jett looked down at his feet. "Carmen's mom sent them to me a while ago."

"Those were supposed to be for me!" I said.

"Really?" he asked. "Well, they fit me better, and GiGi says they look great."

"Yeah, what else does she say?" I lowered my voice to GiGi's (fake) throaty whisper and said, "The Kabbalah is doing such amazing things for Demi's aura. I definitely need to get into that. If only I could read words with more than two syllables."

"Be nice," Jett replied. But behind his look of annoyance I could tell he thought it was funny. Which was cool, and then not. Because if he saw through GiGi, why did he like her so much?

"Dad really wants to go skiing. We should do it."

Jett shrugged. "Whatever, I don't really care."

"Then why can't you just agree with Dad and let him have his ski trip?" I asked. "Why do you always have to take GiGi's side? I mean, where is your loyalty, Jett? He's our father."

I was pretty worked up. Obviously I wasn't talking about our vacation anymore.

Jett should have realized. Or, at least, I *wish* he realized, but instead he shot me a look that made me feel ten inches tall. "How can you defend Dad when he missed Austin's memorial service today and he hasn't even apologized or acknowledged it or anything?"

My brother had a good point, but I wasn't going to tell him so. For some reason my eyes filled up with tears. I wiped them away quickly and slumped down in my seat.

Not only was I all choked up, I was also really upset that I was suddenly all choked up, which just made things worse.

I've been paranoid about crying in public ever since Jett and I went to a Marguerite Mathers Film Festival two years ago on the anniversary of our mom's death. I didn't even see anyone taking my picture, but somehow my tear-streaked face ended up on the cover of *The National Enquirer* the next day, right underneath a shot of Bigfoot's alien baby. I don't know what was more upsetting, the fact that a bunch of kids from school saw me in a moment of weakness and started calling me "poor little rich girl" or the fact that the Bigfoot alien baby's story was five pages long when all I got was one paragraph.

"Sorry, Jazzy." Jett reached across the table and squeezed my arm. "I know this is just as hard for you, since you and Austin had a lot of, um, history."

If Jett was using "history" as a euphemism for "heartache, screaming fights, head games, mutual betrayal, and the occasional moment of true understanding and pure bliss," he was right. But that was merely one small contributing factor to my current crisis.

"I'm fine," I said. "I mean, I'm really upset, but whatever. It's upsetting, you know? And the screenplay thing is . . . well . . ." I couldn't bring myself to say it. Jett would freak, and I didn't want to cause a scene.

"Well, what?" asked Jett.

"All that stuff with Austin got so complicated, and now it's even worse. I have this really bad feeling and it's hard to explain, but—"

"I know what happened," Jett said, interrupting as he raised his dark-eyed gaze to mine. "You don't have to explain anything."

Suddenly my heart started pounding in my ears. Everything started spinning, like the entire restaurant was perched on the DJ's turntable. Jett knew? I couldn't believe that a) Austin had told him I wrote about his and GiGi's affair, and b) he was being so calm about the whole thing. At the same time, it was kind of a relief. Or, at least, nice to know that I wasn't in this alone anymore. "I'm really sorry, Jett. It was an accident."

"Well, that's a strange way to put it, but there's no need to apologize to me," he said, with an easy shrug. "It was your thing."

I was shocked that Jett was being so great about this. And

that he didn't hate me for it. Although maybe it was a relief for him, too. Maybe once things were out in the open, we'd all be better off. "Do you want me to be there when you tell Dad?" I asked. "Or would you rather do it alone?"

Suddenly Jett looked at me like I was crazy. "Why would I tell Dad?"

"Well, his company is about to buy the story, so eventually he'll have to read it. Or do you think it won't make it that far? That's what I'm counting on, but I don't know if we can take the risk. He'll learn the truth eventually, and I think it would be better if he found out from you."

"Huh?" asked Jett.

My voice wavered as I asked, "Wait, what are you talking about?"

Jett sat back and crossed his arms over his chest. "You and Charlie. I know you were cheating on Austin with his brother. And that then later, you cheated on Charlie with Austin. I mean, I suspected something weird was going on, and he then finally told me. The thing you guys had, it was messed up. For two people who were supposedly so in love, you sure treated each other badly."

"Yeah," I agreed quickly. "That's true."

Jett tilted his head to one side and stared at me. "What did you think I was talking about?"

"Nothing," I said, with a quick shake of my head. "There's nothing else."

Jett was waiting for me to say something, but just thinking about this entire mess made me feel claustrophobic.

"Hey, Dad told me you have Austin's screenplay. Can I take a look at it when you're done?" he asked.

My stomach dropped. Why hadn't I thought about that before? Of course Jett would want to see "Austin's" screenplay.

My brother isn't a big reader, but obviously he'd want to check out something his best friend supposedly wrote. I needed an excuse—fast. "Um, sure, but don't you have that paper on Kafka due soon? I know you got an extension, but have you finished your reading for it yet? Because I'd hate for you to get wrapped up in something else and forget about it."

Jett narrowed his eyes at me. "That's none of your business, Jazzy. Stop being such a nag. You're not Carmen. Carmen isn't even Carmen anymore. I'm twenty-one years old, damn it. This is so not cool."

Did I mention my brother has sort of a chip on his shoulder? It's probably because Dad had to build USC a library so they'd let Jett in. And even that didn't stop the dean last month from warning Jett that if he didn't pass enough classes to give him sophomore status this semester, then he wouldn't be able to stay there much longer.

Not that Jett seems to care. He isn't exactly enthusiastic about the whole college experience. Sometimes I forget he's even enrolled, since he's always around.

It's so annoying, having a brother who's supposed to be away at school hanging around the house all the time, blasting his music, eating all the good food, and playing Xbox NHL Hockey obsessively.

Carmen says I need to go easy on him, though. According to her, Jett stays at home so much because he's afraid that if he lets Dad and me out of his sight for too long, he'll lose us. It has something to do with his, *our*, tumultuous childhood. It's more complicated, of course. But unfortunately, Carmen switched her major from psychology to business long ago, so that was all the insight she had to offer.

I probably should try to be more understanding, but sometimes it's hard. Jett could be the coolest, most sensitive and insightful guy one moment and a self-absorbed, obnoxious jerk the next. Plus, the GiGi affair was unforgivable. Especially since Jett could go out with anyone, practically. Lubna is amazing and beautiful and cool and still hung up on him. And girls from USC are always calling. So why did my brother choose the one relationship that had the potential to destroy our father?

And why didn't I confront him when I found out about it three months ago?

Before I had much time to ponder these questions, our waitress came back to the table with our food.

GiGi and Dad returned soon after.

"Justin Riley is so nice. He's completely down to earth," GiGi said, as if we cared. "I'm so glad we ran into him." Before attacking her child-size portion of dinner, she whipped out her cell and called her agent so she could tell him the same thing.

I arched my eyebrows at Jett, but he was too busy drowning his sushi in soy sauce to notice me.

Apparently, my brother was done talking to me for the night. And I guess, in a way, that was a good thing.

Later, when I was alone in my room, I tried to remember when, exactly, everything started with Jett and GiGi. Were there clues in their first meeting? Something I failed to pick up on that first night they met?

CHAPTER SIX

Interior of the Browns' house: a large, airy
entryway with high ceilings. Jess and Jake are
sitting on the second-story landing at the top of
the stairs. Their feet are dangling over the
edge, and their arms are looped through the
wooden rails. Their faces are forlorn, as if
they're peering out from a jail cell.

The camera pans down to the entryway, where
Ginger struggles with a stack of large, bulky
boxes. Neither of them makes a move to help her.
In fact, they whisper so as not to be heard.

                    JESS
          She shouldn't bring so much with her.
          It'll just make it harder for when she
          has to leave.

                    JAKE
          I hope she's kept her old place.
          Remember how Sandy had to live in the
          guesthouse for two months after she
          and Dad split up, just because she

couldn't find a decent rental on the
west side?

                    JESS
God, that was a nightmare.

                    JAKE
So how long do you give this one?

                    JESS
A year, tops. You?

                    JAKE
You're way too generous. My guess is
she's gone in six months.

                    JESS
Do you want to bet?

                    JAKE (nodding)
The usual terms?

Ginger disappears outside and moments later, Alex
walks inside carrying a stack of boxes. Ginger
trails behind him, empty-handed and smiling.

Jess is annoyed. Jake, amused.

                    JAKE
Your boyfriend is so helpful.

                    JESS
Shut up.

Camera pans back downstairs.

                    ALEX
Where do you want these?

                    GINGER
In the master suite.

Alex looks around, clearly struggling with the heavy
boxes.

                    ALEX
I know it's somewhere back past the
office, but which door is it?

                    GINGER (embarrassed)
Oh, I was hoping you'd know.

Jess comes running downstairs and flings herself
into Alex's arms, causing him to drop Ginger's boxes.

                    JESS
You're late.

                    ALEX
I hope none of that was breakable.

                    GINGER
Don't worry about it. Jess, I'm so glad
you're here. Your dad said that you'd
help me get settled.

Jess ignores Ginger and talks to Alex.

                    JESS
We can still make it to Santa Monica if

we hurry. The movie starts at eight
thirty.

                    ALEX

What movie?

                    JESS

I told you I wanted to see the new
Quentin Tarantino movie tonight.

                    GINGER

Oh, you don't have to see that in a
public theater. Your father is showing
it tomorrow night in the screening
room.

                    ALEX

Good. There's this band playing at
Moomba tonight—Death by Flypaper. We
should totally check them out. J. T. is
friends with the bass player and they
might let us open for them at The El
Rey next month.

                    JESS

I'd rather see the movie.

                    ALEX

But Ginger just said your dad is
screening it tomorrow night.

                    JESS

I like seeing movies in real theaters.

GINGER (recoiling)
Why?

JESS
The popcorn is better.

GINGER
Before you go, can you tell me where to
put these boxes?

Jess points to the top of the stairs, where Jake is
watching.

JESS
I can't or we'll be late, but I'm sure
my brother would be more than happy to
help.

Everyone looks up and sees Jake staring down at
them. Busted, Jake stands and stomps down the steps.
He and Alex nod at each other. They are best friends,
so they exchange the standard warm, Southern
California best-guy-friend greeting.

ALEX
Dude.

JAKE
Hey, dude.

Jake bends down and picks up the smallest box in the
entryway and heads off, briskly, toward the back of
the house. Ginger hurries after him, empty-handed.

                        GINGER
I don't think we've met yet. I'm
Ginger Bell.

                    JAKE (MUMBLING)
No shit.

                ALEX (LOOKING WORRIED)
Shouldn't we help her move in?

                        JESS
We're gonna be late for the movie.

                        ALEX
Can't we please go hear music instead?
I promised J. T., and I still owe the
band this since they had to cancel last
summer's tour because of me.

                        JESS
I still can't believe you chose summer
school over music.

                        ALEX
You don't get it. How will I ever get
into medical school with a C-plus in
organic chemistry?

                        JESS
Since when do you even *want* to go to
medical school?

                         ALEX
Can we not have this fight now? Just,
let's go to Moomba tonight and I'll
take you to the movie tomorrow night,
okay?

                         JESS

There's no point in going out to the
movie on the same night it's being
screened here. That's just silly.

                         ALEX
But it's okay to see it the night
before?

                         JESS
Obviously.

                         ALEX
Well, how about this? I'll come over
tomorrow night to watch the movie
with you, and I'll bring some real
movie theater popcorn.

                         JESS
Okay, fine. But I don't want this to
be one of those nights where everyone
but me gets wasted and the music is
awful and too loud and we're all
crammed around some small, sticky table
and shouting over the noise to be heard.

                         ALEX
It won't be like that. I promise.

Cut to: Scene at the bar. Everyone but Jess is wasted, and the music is awful and too loud and everyone is crammed around some small table, shouting over the noise to be heard. Jess lifts her elbow off the table and realizes it's sticky. Worse, she's got peanut shells stuck to the sleeve of her favorite black leather jacket. She makes a face.

Just then Veronica, a small, blond, cheerleader type approaches. She makes the rounds, hugging everyone at the table. When she gets to Alex, she kisses him on both cheeks.

Alex scoots his chair over to make room for Veronica, accidentally pushing Jess off hers.

                    ALEX
          Whoops, sorry.

Alex offers Jess a hand, but she stands up on her own, wiping more peanut shells off the seat of her pants.

                    JESS
          It's cool. I was getting tired of
          sitting.

                    ALEX
          Sorry, babe. Meet Veronica.

          VERONICA (SMILING TOO BRIGHT)
          You're the famous Jess? It's so great
          to finally meet you.

JESS
Who are you?

ALEX
Sorry. Jess, this is Veronica, my
downstairs neighbor. Veronica, meet
Jess, my girlfriend.

VERONICA
Alex has told me so much about you. I
love your mom. I've seen all her movies
and—

JESS (FAKE FRIENDLY)
Me too!

VERONICA (CONFUSED)
She was so glamorous, and you look just
like her. Wow, it's so wild meeting
you. I was just reading about your dad
in *Variety*.

JESS
You read *Variety*?

VERONICA
I'm a film student.

JESS
I need some air.

As Jess leaves, Veronica turns to Alex.

VERONICA

What did I do? How come she hates me?

Jess goes outside to make a phone call.

JESS (INTO THE PHONE)

Chad?

CHAD

Where are you?

JESS

In hell.

CHAD

I'd no idea that hell had such
excellent cell phone reception. Maybe
I should move there.

JESS

Don't bother. I'm leaving. Can you
meet me in twenty minutes?

CHAD

What am I, your boy toy? You think I've
just been waiting by the phone all
night for your call?

JESS

So you're busy?

CHAD

Of course not. I've been waiting by the

phone all night for your call. So where
should we meet?

> JESS

Griffith Park. By the observatory.

Jess hangs up and walks to her car. She's about to
open up the door when Alex runs over. Seeing him, she
turns around.

> ALEX

You're leaving without saying good-bye.

> JESS

Oh, right. Sorry. Bye.

> ALEX

What's up with you?

> JESS

Nothing. I'm just tired. You can get a
ride home, right?

> ALEX

I'll come with.

> JESS

No, don't. You should stay. I know you
want to hear that band. I'm sure Vera
would be happy to drive you back to
school.

> ALEX

You mean Veronica.

                    JESS

Whatever.

                    ALEX

What's wrong? Are you upset about
Ginger?

                    JESS

It's just, like, the same old scene,
you know? I'm sick of it.

                    ALEX

Well, with your dad's track record,
she won't last long.

                    JESS

Thanks a lot.

                    ALEX

What? It's okay for you to make bets
with Jake, but I can't acknowledge the
obvious? How is that fair?

                    JESS

I never said it was fair. It's just,
he's still my father. Plus, if this
marriage ends, there'll be another.
There always is. And isn't the evil I
know better than the evil I don't
know?

Alex leans down to give Jess a kiss.

                         ALEX
     I need to get back inside. I'll see you
     tomorrow, though. Okay?

Waving good-bye, Jess gets into her car.

Cut to a scene of Jess and Chad making out.
They're in front of the Griffith Observatory, in
the Hollywood Hills, sitting on a picnic blanket,
surrounded by food. When they roll onto the
cheese plate, Jess breaks away.

                         JESS
     It's late. I should get home.

                         CHAD
     Ten more minutes.

They continue to make out.

Fade out.

Fade in. It's morning. A dog is licking Jess's
face. She swats it away, rolls over, ends up on
the grass. Opens her eyes. Is shocked.

She and Chad fell asleep in the park. It's
morning. Joggers run by. The dog, a golden
retriever, is sitting, panting, watching. Jess
wakes up Chad. They both gather their things and
head home.

Jess sneaks into her house and hears loud voices.

She heads back to the gym and peeks around the
corner. Her brother and her new stepmom are
bickering.

                        JAKE
          This is my gym.

                        GINGER
          But your father said I could put my
          workout stuff in here.

                        JAKE
          He didn't say that to me. Why don't you
          put your stuff in the garage?

                        GINGER
          It's just a few weights. I don't
          understand what the big deal is.

                        JAKE
          They're pink. You can't put pink
          weights in my gym.

                        GINGER
          Didn't your father tell me you lived on
          campus?

                    JAKE (HYSTERICAL)
          This is still my gym.

Jess rolls her eyes, heads upstairs, and falls into
bed, covering her head with a pillow.

CHAPTER SEVEN

I MUST HAVE FALLEN ASLEEP WHILE READING because the next thing I knew, the sun was blazing through my window, heating up the entire room. I was still in last night's clothes, sweating in my suede jacket. Sitting up, I peeled it off, and that's when I saw it: the crinkled stack of pages resting on my pillow.

The guilt hit me all at once. I'd been acting so selfish. All I'd been worried about was what would happen to my own family if the truth got out. I hadn't even thought about the Coopers. Austin was gone, and I'd cheated on him with his brother. That's so messed up as it is. But to make matters worse, I'd made him look like a boneheaded alcoholic in the screenplay. If word got out that I wrote the screenplay and it wasn't exactly a work of fiction, his parents would figure out that Austin was Alex and that Charlie was Chad. That would leave them completely horrified and humiliated, and it wasn't fair. They shouldn't have to be put through that, because they've been through enough already.

The thing is, even though I didn't lie or exaggerate and my depiction of him was painfully accurate, I'd only written about Austin's worst side, the guy he'd turned into at the end of our relationship.

He wasn't always like that. If he had been, I never would have fallen for him in the first place. But Austin was the first guy I ever liked in that heart-fluttering, nervous-stuttering, writing-his-name-all-over-my-notebook kind of way.

He and Jett were best friends, and when we were younger, he was always at our house. I saw him more often than I saw our cat, Gladys. (Although I see lots of people more often than I see Gladys, who spends most of her time under Jett's bed, and only comes out to eat in the middle of the night.)

It used to be that I'd think up any excuse to spend time with him: Austin, will you help me study for my math test? Austin, I just rented *Star Wars*. Do you want to watch it with me? Austin, I just hung this signed, framed picture of Pavement above my bed. Will you come and see if it looks crooked to you? Oh, you love Pavement too? I had no idea. . . .

At some point near the end of my freshman year, I realized that Austin was coming up with excuses to hang with me, too: Jasmine, do you need help studying for your math test? Jasmine, Jett is going out tonight and I didn't realize and brought over *Say Anything*. Do you want to watch it with me? Jasmine, they gave me an extra Ultimo Burrito at Baja Fresh. Do you want it? Oh, you love Ultimo Burritos with savory pork carnitas too? I had no idea. . . .

We finally got together that summer, right before he started college. That first year we were together was amazing. Austin was my first boyfriend, and sometimes I felt like dating him propelled me into a higher stratosphere. Music sounded better. Colors seemed brighter, and ice cream tasted sweeter.

He was going to be a rock star, and in a sense, he already was. He had this fire inside him, this amazing energy that radiated. Not just when he was onstage either. I mean all the time.

So when I was with Austin, things that normally bugged me

didn't. Dad and his then-wife Simrin were fighting up a storm, but I couldn't have cared less. Lubna had abandoned me for college up north, but it wasn't a big deal. Carmen told me she was looking for a place of her own, and at the time, I felt like I could handle it. As Austin Cooper's girlfriend, I had it all.

We had it all because we had each other. I know that sounds corny, but it's true.

I don't know when, exactly, things went bad. But they did, and it felt sudden. Like one day Austin woke up and turned off the switch. The fire disappeared.

Looking back, I realize that the change *wasn't* drastic. That actually, things had started to fall apart last summer. Austin's band had made big plans to go on tour for the months of July and August. T. J. found an old van to rent, and they'd all worked hard to book a bunch of gigs at small clubs in tiny cities all over the country.

Austin was completely stoked, until he got his grades for the semester. Turns out, he'd gotten a C-plus in organic chemistry. His parents freaked, claiming that no medical school would ever accept him. They pressured him to take the class over again in summer school, and he caved. Canadian Bacon had to cancel the whole tour. T. J. and the rest of the band were surprisingly cool about it. They managed to secure a few local gigs at The El Rey instead, but suddenly Austin was too busy even for that.

Things were a mess. But even after it was over between us, neither of us wanted it to end. It was as if our relationship had an expiration date and we'd sailed past it without noticing. We'd become old milk with sour chunks floating around inside, but we held our noses and closed our eyes and continued to sip because we wanted to pretend it still tasted delicious.

I wanted him back, which is why I showed him my diary back in October.

Not the whole thing. At first, I just fed him the scene from his parents' anniversary party so he'd understand how awful he'd been, drinking too much and flirting with GiGi right in front of me.

The weird thing was that rather than be upset or insulted, he really liked it. He wanted to see more, so I handed over the scene from the club where I first met Violet. He didn't even care that I made him look like a jerk. He was over the fact that I'd been sneaking around with Charlie.

He thought it was funny.

He was entertained.

I'd created something that Austin thought was cool. It was a rush.

So I printed out the whole thing and slapped on a title: *Cold Blooded, Two-Timing Rat.* At the time, I told myself it was so he'd understand who he'd become and go back to who he was. In a twisted way, I thought reading my diary might help.

At least that's what I told myself. Maybe my real reasons were more selfish. Maybe I was just looking for his approval. Because I certainly loved hearing him sing my praise.

Austin had only had the screenplay for a week before he died. It's crazy that he's getting credit for writing it. I'm not even sure he found the time to read the whole thing.

Of course, none of that mattered anymore. Austin was gone, and that was the worst thing. Nothing was going to change that. I needed to stop obsessing.

I was blowing this whole deal way out of proportion. Just because Dr. Cooper announced that EggBrite was buying the screenplay didn't mean it would actually happen. My dad told me the deal wasn't done, and deals fell through all the time. Even if the studio did buy the screenplay, there was only a slim chance that the movie would actually get made.

I was worrying for nothing.

So I hid the screenplay back under my bed, took a shower, and headed downstairs.

GiGi was at the kitchen table, wearing a pink silk bathrobe and sipping her usual breakfast, which she called a fruit smoothie even though it was actually just water, crushed ice, and a small squeeze of lemon.

Oddly, she was looking down at the *L.A. Times* with great interest. Usually she only reads *Us Weekly*. (Although, honestly, I'm pretty sure that she only subscribes for the pictures.)

"Hi, Jasmine. How did you sleep?" she asked.

Barely grunting, I headed for the coffeemaker and poured myself a cup. GiGi is a morning person, and she keeps forgetting that I'm not. When I wake up I feel like my body is wrapped in invisible layers of gauze, separating me from the rest of the world. People can talk at me, but nothing will penetrate until I am sufficiently caffeinated.

"Your dad had to leave early, but he wanted me to ask you about Ixtapa," she went on.

I looked at her blankly. "Ixtapa?"

"Ixtapa, Mexico. For our vacation next week."

"Wait. What happened to skiing?" I sat down next to her and blinked. Trying to clear my head, I took another sip of coffee, then rubbed my eyes.

"I really need to work on my tan, and your dad says Hawaii is too far," GiGi explained.

Last week, she'd had a tanning bed installed in the garage, between her makeshift gym and Dad's temperature and humidity-controlled wine closet, but I didn't bother arguing.

"What are you reading?" I asked instead.

"There's an article about Austin in the Calendar section of today's paper."

As I zoomed in on the headline I almost spit out a mouthful of coffee:

REBEL WITH A CAUSE AND A LAPTOP: HOLLYWOOD'S HOTTEST YOUNG WRITER, GONE BEFORE HIS TIME

"Are you okay?" asked GiGi, in reaction to my bug-eyed stupor.

"Um, do you mind?" I managed to choke out as I pulled the paper from GiGi's hands and started reading.

Rock-'n'-roll legends Janis Joplin, Jim Morrison, and Jimi Hendrix all died of drug overdoses at the age of twenty-seven.

Painter Jean-Michel Basquiat also died at the age of twenty-seven, of a heroine overdose.

For actor River Phoenix, it was a combination of crystal meth, cocaine, and heroine, when he was twenty-three.

The drugs may have changed, but the story has not. Many brilliant young artists have traveled down this tragic path before. And, sadly, it's time to add a new name to the list.

Screenwriter Austin Cooper overdosed at the age of nineteen.

After dropping two hits of Ecstasy and then consuming copious amounts of alcohol, Austin Cooper collapsed on the sidewalk in front of Club Moomba, and never got up again.

The UCLA sophomore was more than just another drug-and-alcohol-related casualty of Sunset Boulevard's late-night party scene. He was one of Hollywood's most talented young scribes, but no one knew it until it was too late.

How does one explain the link between alcohol, recreational drug use, creative genius, and early death? Why do so many bright young stars succumb to these dangerous temptations?

Marvin Green, the president of EggBrite Studios (whose first wife, Marguerite Mathers, also died before she hit thirty), dodged the question. "Austin Cooper had talent, plain and simple. It's tragic that his life ended at such a tender age, but I'm relieved that his gem of a screenplay was unearthed. Here at EggBrite Studios we're thrilled to have the opportunity to produce his story. The writing is brilliant, and that's not a term I throw around. We're in the middle of casting and we're going to start filming any day now."

No doubt, the studio will put all of their resources behind making sure the movie is a hit. They may have won the fierce bidding war, but it didn't come cheaply. Rumor has it that EggBrite spent somewhere in the one-million-dollar range for the rights—a staggering amount for a first-time screenwriter of any age.

How does Austin's family feel about his sudden, posthumous success? Austin's mother, Dr. Lori Cooper, says, "Even though my eldest son is gone, I take comfort in the fact that his artistic vision will live on."

Girlfriend and fellow UCLA student Violet Peterson tries to remain positive. "I truly believe that Austin Cooper was my soul mate and that I will never love again. We were a great couple. I always encouraged him and I never got in the way of his creative process. I'm thrilled that his work is going to come to life, though saddened that he didn't live to see the day. Still, it's true what they say: Every cloud has a silver lining."

By the time I finished the article, my whole body was trembling. And it wasn't just because of Violet's sloppy use of weak clichés.

Here was my dad, raving about Austin's talent to the *L.A. Times*, when he hadn't even read a word of the screenplay. And here was Violet, acting as if she knew Austin was writing all along, when he wasn't.

I could have put a stop to this yesterday, but I was too much of a wimp. Now it was too late.

As much as I didn't want to believe it was the case, I had to face facts. My movie, "Austin's movie," was going to get made. The truth would come out, no question about it.

I was in trouble, big-time. We all were.

I felt GiGi's hand on my arm. "I'm sorry, honey," she said. "I know what Austin meant to you and Jett. It's a horrible thing you have to go through."

I barely managed to mumble a reply. For all of GiGi's faults, which are many, she isn't terrible. Forgetting about the major issue, she's not the worst stepmom I've ever had. She doesn't try to be a parent or my best friend, like some of them have. She lets me come and go as I please, without asking too many questions. She cleans up after herself too, making her more like a very polite houseguest.

She's not the one who'll be responsible for the public mortification of our entire family. No, that's all my fault.

"What's wrong with you?" asked Jett.

Simple question. Complicated answer.

As my brother slouched his way into the kitchen, all my warm and fuzzy feelings for GiGi vanished. GiGi didn't turn around when he came into the room, but she did sit up straighter and subtly track him with her gaze. Even though she was wearing a bathrobe, as if she'd just rolled out of bed, she was already in full makeup.

"They wrote about Austin in the *L.A. Times*," said GiGi, pointing to the paper.

"Seriously? Let me see." Jett swiped the paper out from under my nose and scanned the piece. When he finished, he asked, "Jasmine, you still have the screenplay, right? Are you almost done with it?"

"No," I replied quickly as I pulled myself to my feet. "I just started. In fact, I think I'm going to go read it, now."

I ran upstairs and closed and locked the door behind me. For once, I was glad that Jett and GiGi were so wrapped up in each other, because it meant they wouldn't notice me freaking out.

I can't believe I didn't tell my dad the truth last night, when I'd had the chance. Now it was too late. If there was any way of pulling the plug on this movie, it sure wasn't obvious to me. I needed help.

Carmen was still in El Salvador, and Lubna was in London. But today was the day that my friend Duke would be coming home from visiting his dad in New York.

I dialed his cell and was so thrilled when he picked up, I blurted out, "Are you back yet?" before I even said hello.

Duke laughed and said, "My plane just landed."

I glanced around my messy room in search of my car keys. "Can I come over?" I asked.

"Sure, I'll call you when I get home."

"That's okay," I said as I pulled on the first pair of jeans I found on my floor. "I'm leaving now. I'll meet you there, okay?"

"Um, okay," said Duke. "But what's the hurry?"

"Long story," I replied as I stepped into my flip-flops. "Better if I tell you in person."

CHAPTER EIGHT

TEN MINUTES LATER I WAS SPEEDING DOWN SUNSET Boulevard, heading toward Duke's place in Malibu. Since Duke has the distinction of being my only friend who is still alive, still in the country, *and* still speaking to me, I was thrilled that he was home. I was also feeling hopeful for the first time since I found out about this whole mess.

Duke is awesome. We've been practically inseparable ever since the day we met last year in tenth grade, when he accidentally called me an evil bitch to my face. Yeah, seriously, but it totally wasn't his fault.

Let me explain: Duke transferred to Bel Air Prep halfway through our sophomore year, and Dee-Ann Williams (who hates me) was assigned to be his "student-escort." (I know. It's crazy that our school's administration hasn't figured out that the word "escort" has some very unseemly connotations.)

Anyway, as a "student-escort," Dee-Ann was tasked with showing Duke where all of his classes were, introducing him around, and eating lunch with him on his first day of school. She also took it upon herself to give him the dirt on everyone she knew. Among other salacious tidbits, she told him that Caleb Samuels gets high in the back of his van every morning. Meredith

Bennet throws up every day after lunch. Dustin Pedral had a nose job. And Jasmine Green is a spoiled brat, with her own car and driver.

Pretty harsh, right? The thing is, she was right about me. Not the spoiled brat part; the other thing.

Until I got my license, I was shuttled to and from school by a private driver. However, it's not like I had any choice in the matter. By the time I started at Bel Air Prep, Jett had been kicked out. He was doing his senior year at a school on the other side of town, so he couldn't drive me. Neither could my dad, who takes breakfast meetings at least three mornings a week. Carmen had just started graduate school, and most of her classes met in the a.m. There's no bus that goes to my school, it's too far to walk, and I was in between stepmoms. How else was I supposed to get there?

I'm not even the only kid at Bel Air Prep who has or who once had a driver. (I can name three others.) I am, however, the only kid with a driver who also had Mick Jagger perform at her sixteenth birthday party.

The story made *People* magazine and a week later, I found the article, with pictures, taped to my locker. I guess enough people saw it before I tore it down and ripped it to shreds, because word got out. Those friends I'd thought I had now shunned me in the halls.

The real irony is, I'm not even that into the Rolling Stones. When I was younger and Mick came to our house, all fat lips and leathery skin, he used to scare me. But he happens to be a good friend of my dad's, so I'd never complain. It's not like my dad even asked him to perform. He just decided to play a few songs at the last minute, but that was enough to cement my reputation.

That, and the party itself. It was a surprise, so I had no say about who was invited. Bonnie, my dad's then-girlfriend, invited only A-list celebrities. So although there were two hundred people in attendance, no one I actually hung out with was there. Everyone from school thought I'd purposely kept them off the list, so I came across looking like a mega-bitch.

The whole age thing didn't help matters either. I'm a year older than my classmates, not because I was held back on purpose but because Dad forgot to enroll me in kindergarten when I was five. It was only when Carmen moved in and asked why I wasn't in school that anyone realized I was supposed to be. She fought the school district, hoping I could skip, but they wouldn't let me. So I became the girl with the driver, and the over-the-top, super-exclusive birthday parties, who's so dumb, she was held back in kindergarten.

Once this all got out, no one in my grade at Bel Air Prep would have anything to do with me. Luckily, I wasn't left completely alone that year. Lubna was a senior and perfectly happy letting me hang out with her friends. But when she graduated, I felt abandoned. First semester of sophomore year, I was stuck eating lunch by myself, reading and/or listening to tunes on my iPod.

Then Duke came along. By his second day, Dee-Ann had determined that his "cool-factor" was in the negative numbers, so she ditched him. This was before she found out that he was gay. Once she realized, she tried to be his best friend because she was convinced that having a gay friend made you extra cool, but it was too late. Duke saw right through that.

Anyway, when I noticed Duke eating lunch in the cafeteria by himself, it was too sad. I couldn't stand it.

Plus, I saw that he was reading *The Great Gatsby*, which is one of my favorite books. I knew he was a sophomore, and that the book wasn't required reading until our junior year. Any guy who reads F. Scott Fitzgerald for fun was definitely someone I wanted to know.

Sitting down across from him, I told him that some scholars believe that *The Great Gatsby* was actually based on an idea that the novelist's wife, Zelda Fitzgerald, had. Duke had read the same thing, so we got to talking. It turned out that we both loved Hemingway, Kafka, and (secretly) Madonna's *The Immaculate Collection.*

When I finally got around to asking him about what he thought of Bel Air Prep, he said it was fine and nothing new. That he'd transferred from a school in New York with plenty of spoiled rich kids. Also, in New York, he'd even known someone who was as outrageous as the infamous Jasmine Green.

I asked him what he'd heard about her, and he'd yawned and said, "Oh, you know. The usual. She's an evil bitch, and her dad hired the Rolling Stones to play at her fifteenth birthday party."

"Actually, it was her sixteenth," I said. "And he performed for free because he's a friend of the family."

"Whatever," said Duke. "It's still crazy. Dee-Ann told me her dad paid to have the school build an Olympic-size swimming pool just so she'd get accepted."

(Technically, Dad had paid for the pool, but it was so they'd let Jett in. My grades and test scores were good enough on their own. But I didn't correct him this time.)

We kept on talking about me until my English teacher, Mr. Azner, walked by and said, "Hi, Jasmine."

Duke stopped talking mid-sentence and his face turned various shades of pink and then he looked at me, as if for confirmation. I nodded and held out my hand. "Jasmine Green, Evil Bitch, at your service."

Then we both just lost it, laughing like hyenas and causing such a ruckus that Dee-Ann and all of her friends shot us dirty looks from across the cafeteria.

It's been almost a year since then, and Duke has finally

stopped apologizing. Not that he ever needed to. Thinking about that lunch still cracks me up.

I got to Duke's place before he made it home from the airport, but that wasn't a big deal. I was happy to wait for him outside on his front lawn, in the shade of one of the eucalyptus trees. I could hear the ocean waves crashing behind me, and it was a clear, sunny day.

Duke lives in Point Dume, Malibu, in the nicest trailer park you've ever seen. Two years ago his mom left his dad, and their sprawling Park Avenue apartment in New York City, to move to Malibu because she wanted to get away from all the materialism and snobbery of New York. The idea was to reinvent herself—to transform from an uptight society matron into a free-thinking, counterculture hippie.

She tried really hard, trading in all of her Chanel suits for flowy skirts and peasant blouses. Still, her plan wasn't completely successful since the trailer park is filled with other rich people who wanted to drop out of society—but not so much that they didn't still drive BMWs and fancy SUVs and keep their day jobs. Sure, the trailers were smaller than most of the houses in my neighborhood, but they were just as nice looking, with Tuscan or Cape Cod–style fronts, and fancy palm tree and cacti landscaping. Plus, they had better views. I could see both the Pacific Ocean and the Santa Monica Mountains from Duke's front yard. It was awesome.

No wonder that for every old-time hippie living there, there were two lawyers. Also in residence were two soap opera stars, a professional skateboarder, and this trustafarian surfer dude who was the heir to some big toilet seat company.

None of this bothers Sunshine, though. (Duke's mom makes us call her that even though her real name is Evelyn.) She pretends like the park is this fabulously unique place, where no one has or needs money because they all have such great energy.

Duke isn't convinced, but he likes California better than New York, and living with his mom is easier than living with his dad, who's kind of uptight.

Anyway, he must have hit a lot of traffic because fifteen minutes went by before I saw Duke's familiar blue hybrid come around the bend. I ran over and flung myself into his arms as soon as he got out of his car.

"You have no idea how much I missed you," I said, burying my face in his neck and squeezing his familiar, slightly chubby frame.

He laughed. "So I gathered. I missed you, too. Stress much?"

"Yes."

Pulling away, he straightened his round glasses and blinked at me with his big brown eyes. His normally long and shaggy, bleached-blond hair was slicked back.

I combed my fingers through it, pushing his bangs back on his forehead, where they belonged. "How much product did you use this morning? Your hair feels so stiff."

Duke backed away and swatted at my hand. "Cut it out. I'm going for a new look here."

"Well, I like the old look."

"You're not the boss of me," he said, but he let me finish fixing his hair, anyway. When I was through, my hand was sticky and as I wiped it on my jeans I wrinkled my nose. This didn't go unnoticed.

"Very funny," Duke said. "So, are you okay? Sorry I wasn't at Austin's service."

"It's okay. I mean, it was really hard, but I know you tried to make it." Unlike my dad, Duke actually had a good excuse for not being there. He has to spend part of every school break in New York, and his father wouldn't let him leave early.

"Did you have breakfast yet?" Duke asked, slinging his duffel bag over his shoulder and heading for the trailer.

"I had coffee," I replied, following him inside.

"That's not breakfast."

He was right. I was so upset about everything, I'd forgotten to eat. No wonder I felt hollow inside. No, wait, that's because I'm a horrible, rotten person who sold out herself and her entire family, all in the name of entertainment. I mean therapy.

Lucky for me, Duke is an amazing cook.

"Where's Sunshine?" I asked as he pulled a package of bacon out of the mini-fridge. (Duke's mom is a vegetarian, and he's only allowed to cook meat when she's not home. Even then, he has to burn sage in the house afterward, to cleanse the place of the dead animal smell.)

"She's on some yoga retreat in Costa Rica," Duke said as he placed the cast-iron frying pan on the stovetop. "She needed to align her body with her spirit before the holidays."

"When will she finish being aligned?"

"By tomorrow afternoon," he said. "Stay over, if you want."

"Maybe I will." I sat down at the kitchen table. "How was your dad's?"

"Typical," Duke said as he dropped a few slices of bacon in the pan, then stepped back as the fat sizzled. "So what's going on with you?"

I shrugged and fiddled with the incense in the center of the table. I wasn't looking at Duke but could feel him watching me. Yes, I'd rushed over to his place with grandiose plans of confessing, but now that we were face-to-face, it wasn't that easy. Clearly, Duke could tell that I wasn't ready to talk about why I was so upset, and he wasn't going to push it.

He's cool that way. All through breakfast, he talked about his trip to New York and his weird lunch with his ex-boyfriend, and some new dive bar that he found that doesn't card. He didn't ask me why I was so freaked out, and for a little while I was able to pretend like everything was normal and that my whole world wasn't on the verge of exploding.

After we'd finished eating, we went to his room because he wanted to check his e-mail.

I'd brought the screenplay with me and was just pulling it out of my bag so I could explain what happened when Duke said, "Guess who's been logging lots of hours online?"

Knowing exactly who he was talking about, I had to smile. Mr. Stark is our math teacher, who keeps an online blog that he writes in almost daily. Like most blogs out there in cyberspace, it's so boring, it makes you want to scream until your throat hurts and your ears ring. All he does is ramble on about his glory days as a high school football star in Texas, back when "great bands like Whitesnake" topped the charts. He also includes random stuff like his disdain for hip-hop music and Krispy Kreme doughnuts, which is crazy. What those Krispy Kreme people do with sugar and grease is magical.

If he was any other teacher, we'd totally feel sorry for him, but Mr. Stark is not a good guy. To put it bluntly, he's a homophobic jerk. In between his lectures he blathers on about politics, and his views are not just scary-conservative. They're "guy in a cabin in Montana, who's one step away from sending a letter bomb" frightening. He actually said one day that gay couples shouldn't have the same rights as married ones because the Constitution doesn't recognize marriage between same-sex couples.

When Duke raised his hand to point out that, actually, the Constitution says nothing about marriage, and that if he's using the Constitution as a benchmark, it also says some interesting things about slavery and a woman's right to vote, Mr. Stark gave him a detention.

We complained to the headmaster, who had a talk with Mr. Stark, but it only stopped his ridiculous rantings for a week.

So Duke took matters into his own hands, fighting bigotry with his most successful weapon: mockery. His whole plan was ingenious.

I'd even written about it in my diary.

Which meant it was a part of the screenplay.

Shit.

This wasn't happening. It couldn't be.

A sick feeling crept over me. It was something that was becoming way too common these days.

"Hey, what's that?" Duke asked as I tried to surreptitiously slip the bound pages back into my bag.

"Nothing," I replied.

"Something's up," said Duke, blinking at me. "So why are you so upset?"

"I'm not," I blurted out. "And I need to go." I stood up and hugged my bag to my chest.

"You just got here," said Duke.

"I mean I need to pee." I fled his bedroom, taking all of my baggage—both literal and figurative—with me.

Once I locked myself in the tiny bathroom across the hall, I sat down on the edge of the tub and dropped my head in my hands.

How could I possibly explain this to Duke? Hey, I needed a subplot for my diary, and your life made for great material.

No way would that excuse fly.

Because who puts subplots in their diary?

No one.

This was bad. And once he found out what I'd written, it was only going to get worse.

CHAPTER NINE

Jess and Luke are studying in Luke's bedroom, which is decorated with sports paraphernalia. (Note to self: Research sports paraphernalia. What is it? Posters? Clothing? Those giant hands with the pointing finger? Do jocks still hang pennants on their walls? Or did that just happen on *The Brady Bunch*?)

Jess is sitting on the floor, leaning against the wall, with a book propped up on her bent knees. Luke is lying on his bed, tossing a baseball in the air as they talk. It's a World Series edition signed by Mickey Mantle. (Note to self: Make sure Mickey Mantle is actually a baseball player. If not, substitute with another, confirmed baseball player. Kobe Bryant?)

(Character note: Luke is tall, athletic, and gorgeous, a natural blond, with a great body. Also, he's gay.)

                    LUKE
Stop beating yourself up over this.

You're not the first girl to cheat on
her boyfriend.

                    JESS
With his brother.

                    LUKE
It's better than cheating on him with
his best friend.

                    JESS
Really? You think?

                    LUKE
Of course. Chad is much cuter than
J. T. Smarter, too.

                    JESS
I thought you meant that it was better
morally, somehow.

                    LUKE
No, morally, you're screwed. But
think about it this way: You were
going to break up with him, anyway,
right? So your only problem has to
do with timing.

                    JESS
Sure, that justification is really
going to fly. Alex, I'm sorry I kissed
your brother. I'm sorry your brother
and I have been sneaking around for
six weeks now. I'm sorry I've had a

crush on Chad since the day he started
tutoring me for the SATs back in June.
The laws of physics are at fault. It's
only cheating because I can't break
the time space continuum, and travel
back to keep our relationship from
ever happening.

                    LUKE
That's not what I meant. And when did
you turn into such a sci-fi geek?

                    JESS
Since Chad. He's so nerdy, he's hot.

                    LUKE
I'm only going to say this once. If you
ever speak to me in Klingon, we can't
be friends anymore.

                    JESS
That's fair.

                    LUKE
Why are you obsessing about this,
anyway?

                    JESS
I don't know. I just wish I'd never
gone out with Alex in the first place.

                    LUKE
Bullshit. Last winter you were
smitten.

                              JESS
          Well, things are different now. He's
          changed. And last year I hardly knew
          Chad. Why do they have to be brothers?

                              LUKE
          Speaking of our math teacher . . .

Luke gets up and walks over to his computer.

                              JESS
          We weren't.

                              LUKE
          I know, but I'm bored with this.
          You're over Alex. You're in love with
          Chad. You're in agony. It's been the
          same old story with you for weeks now.
          I've got it. Will you just deal with it
          so we can move on?

                              JESS
          You're so mean.

                              LUKE
          I'm just being honest. You need that.
          Also, I keep forgetting to show you Mr.
          Blunt's blog.

                              JESS
          Why does our math teacher have a blog?

                              LUKE
          To help spread his crazy, lunatic,

right-wing message. Take a look.

     JESS (READING OVER LUKE'S SHOULDER)
"These are dangerous times, and our
country needs to defend its borders.
We should reinstate the draft, but
lower the age to sixteen. I teach high
school, and let me tell you, those
kids are old enough to defend their
country." Wow, this guy is sick!

         LUKE
You're missing the best part. Listen
to what he wrote two days ago. "My
greatest wish is to meet a woman
who shares my values. She also has to
be leggy and blond. No porkers,
please."

         JESS
Disgusting.

         LUKE
I think we should help him out.

         JESS
What do you mean?

         LUKE
Let me call myself . . . Lucy.

         JESS
Wait, you're actually writing to him?

                              LUKE
I'm not. Lucy is.

                              JESS
And what makes you think he'll
respond?

                              LUKE
I'll tell him I'm a Victoria's Secret
model. I'll even send a picture.

                              JESS
Won't he recognize everyone in the
catalog? I'm sure that's his favorite
reading material.

                              LUKE
Not after I change some details with
Photoshop. How does this sound? "Dear
Steve, I was cruising the personals
and I found your site. You are so
right. Gay people shouldn't be allowed
in the military, but I'll take things
one step further. I don't think that
gay people should be allowed to vote,
either. In fact, maybe we should send
them all to Canada."

                              JESS
Are you really going to send him that?

                              LUKE
Think of it as a psychological
experiment. I'm just trying to

better understand how people like
him think.

                    JESS
Like, for the good of mankind?

                    LUKE
No, purely for the entertainment
value.

                    JESS
Isn't pretending to be a woman to
bait our math teacher similar to
identity fraud? Couldn't you get
into a lot of trouble for this?

                    LUKE
It's not like I'm stealing his credit
card number to go on a shopping
spree. And what? You're suddenly so
ethical now? Who is it who's cheating
on her boyfriend? Why can't I
remember her name?

                    JESS
That's it. I can't take it anymore.
I'm breaking up with him.

                LUKE (TEASING)
Those words sound so familiar.
I almost feel as if I'd heard them
before. It's eerie.

                         JESS
             Come on, Luke. Give me a break.
             I mean it this time. I'm really going
             to do it.

                         LUKE
             So do it.

Jess stands up and checks her watch.

                         JESS
             He should be getting out of Bio in
             fifteen minutes, and if I leave now,
             I'll be in his dorm room in half an
             hour.

Jess walks out of Luke's room, determined.

             LUKE (FOCUSED ON HIS COMPUTER)
             You go, girl.

Cut to: Jess in college dorm, walking down the hall.
She knocks, but no one answers. The music from
inside is blaring.

                         JESS
             Hello? Alex? Are you there?

She tries the doorknob and it's open, so she
walks inside. Alex is in bed with another woman.
It's Veronica, the girl from the club. Jess runs
out of the room, in shock. Alex follows, his
lower half wrapped in a towel.

                    ALEX
        Wait, Jess? Come back. This isn't
        what you think. I can explain.

A tearful Jess runs to the parking lot. Alex
chases her outside. Before she gets into her car
she turns around and looks at Alex.

A crowd has gathered and everyone stares.

                    JESS
        You couldn't have at least put on a
        pair of pants?

CHAPTER TEN

I STOPPED READING. IT WAS TOO PAINFUL, AND I'M
not even talking about the nightmarish "walking in on Austin
and Violet in bed" scene. As awful as that had been at the time,
once I'd gotten over the initial shock, I'd felt relieved. Somehow
Austin's cheating made my cheating look better, or at least not
completely evil, you know?

What's so difficult to read about now is all that Luke and Mr.
Blunt business.

Duke really has been cyber-stalking our math teacher, Mr.
Stark. It's been going on for more than three months now. Once
people figure it out, he'll get expelled from school.

Ever since our school's basketball coach and this senior met
in some chat room and started having an affair, our school has
had a very strict and unforgiving policy about the Internet.
Teachers and students can only communicate with one another
online via the school's intranet, which is randomly patrolled by
the administration. Any e-mail sent off the intranet has to be
reported by both the teacher and student immediately. A second
infraction by the sender will result in expulsion or job termina-
tion. As our headmaster made very clear when he created this
policy, no exceptions would be tolerated.

Pretending to be a woman to bait our math teacher and trick him into spilling his deepest, darkest secrets and desires online? Yeah, that's not going to end well for Duke. And worse, when he gets kicked out of school, his dad will probably make him move back to New York.

Duke would hate that.

And how will I survive after my best friend is shipped across the country? I still have a year and a half left at Bel Air Prep. If Duke leaves, who will I hang out with?

And here I go again, on the verge of destroying yet another life, and I can only think of myself.

It's too bad I had to include that one small cyber-stalking scene in the screenplay, because he'd have loved the rest of it.

Duke is always complaining about the way gay men are portrayed in the media. He's sick of seeing them cast in movies and on TV as the campy sidekick, always at the beck and call of some attractive, straight woman with a fabulous career in fashion or public relations. It's as if the archetypical male homosexual is reduced to an accessory, not that different from a Kate Spade purse or a pair of designer shoes. (Got the bag and the $200 haircut, the $500 pair of spike-heeled boots, now what am I missing? My gay sidekick. . . . Now, where did I leave him?)

Yes, Duke is gay, but he never speaks in sarcastic quips. He likes nice clothes but, like me, he's not obsessed with shopping or labels, and he hates going to the gym. From all the self-deprecating remarks he makes about his weight, it's obvious that he wishes he were a little less chubby, which is why I gave him such a great body. His screenplay alter ego is also a naturally blond jock who hates disco and folk music. (Even though, as I already mentioned, we both love Madonna and he's the one who turned me on to Joni Mitchell.)

Unfortunately, all these positive aspects don't change the basic fact that my work is going to sabotage yet another person

I care about. Even though Mr. Stark is the one with seriously toxic political views, in the end, Duke is the one who's going to suffer. It's so unfair. And it's all my fault.

When Duke knocked on the door, I called, "Hold on a minute," and hoped my voice didn't sound too panicky.

"Are you okay?" he asked.

I didn't know how much time had passed, but it must have been a while because he sounded worried.

As much as I wanted to camp out in the bathroom forever, I knew I couldn't. Taking a deep breath, I stood up and splashed some cold water on my teary, weary-eyed, too-puffy face. It didn't do much, but I figured I had plenty of other excuses for being upset today—ones I could actually talk about.

Opening the door, I mumbled an apology. "Sorry. I think everything just caught up with me, you know? The memorial service, thinking about Austin . . . It was really tough seeing everyone."

"It's okay. I can't imagine how hard it was. And is Charlie still refusing to speak to you?"

I nodded. "He wouldn't even look at me. When I entered the room, our eyes met and I waved and he turned away and headed in the other direction, like I'm his Kryptonite."

Back in Duke's room, perched on the edge of his bed, I was careful to keep my bag by my feet.

Duke sat down at his desk and spun his chair around so he was facing me. "I think I know what else is bothering you. You're upset about Austin's screenplay, right?"

A funny noise erupted from my lips—sort of a half gasp, half whimper. "How did you know about that?" I asked.

"I read about it on the plane. There was an article in the *Times*. I saw your dad's quote, too. I'm sure it's hard, having him suddenly so interested in Austin's work."

"What's that supposed to mean?" I asked.

"I don't know." Duke shrugged. "He never cared about Austin when he was alive. The dude practically lived at your house and your dad couldn't even keep his name straight. You always complained that he called him Alex half the time, right?"

I cringed. "It's not his fault. My dad meets tons of people all the time, so it's hard for him to remember names. And he cares now. That's all that matters, right? I mean, my dad is totally innocent in this."

"What do you mean, innocent?" asked Duke.

"Um, nothing. I didn't mean anything."

Duke stared at me. "Are you sure you're okay?" he asked.

"I'm fine." I nodded, perhaps too vigorously.

"Okay, fine. You don't have to tell me. But you did get the maps printed up, right?"

"Maps?" I asked.

"For economics," he reminded me. "We're supposed to have our product ready to launch on the first day of spring semester. That means we have to bring all the inventory to school, remember?"

Oh, right. How could I forget? All semester in economics we've been working on developing small businesses centered around a single product, and Duke and I are partners.

Some students had created a new energy drink. Others were working on a body glitter that doubled as a nail polish. Dee-Ann and her friends were building an exclusive dating website—accessible only to models and other beautiful people.

Duke and I had created an Anti-Star Map, which is the antithesis of those Star Maps people sell to tourists on Hollywood Boulevard. You know the ones—street maps listing the addresses of and directions to the homes of Arnold Schwarzenegger and Jennifer Aniston and to the former homes of Cary Grant, Marilyn Monroe, and my mother. In our version, we only list people tangentially related to the stars: *See where Courtney Love's manicurist lives! Visit Brad Pitt's garbage man! Jessica Simpson once bought a halter top from the woman who lives here!*

I figured that if my mom's old shoes went for three thousand dollars on eBay, people would definitely pay fifteen bucks for our map, which has full-color illustrations designed by yours truly. (Okay, they're stick figures, but people don't buy maps for the art.)

When we announced our idea to the class, our teacher, Ms. Fitzpatrick, claimed we were trying to make a joke out of the whole assignment, which is so not true. So we needed to work extra hard to prove her wrong.

I was supposed to have the maps ready by the time Duke got home from New York. But obviously I was somewhat preoccupied.

"I forgot," I said. "Sorry."

"That's okay," said Duke. "I have all the files here. Let me just burn a new disc and we'll go to Kinko's."

I stood up and said, "I can't. I need to get home."

As I headed for the door, Duke followed me. "But you just got here."

"Yeah," I said. "But I just remembered there's all this stuff I have to do. You know, for the annual Green Family Christmas Party. It's two days away."

"Why do you have to worry about that?"

"Because GiGi just fired the housekeeping staff, and she can't handle it all on her own."

"That sucks," he said.

"Yeah, well . . ." Keeping my head down, I pretended to dig around in my bag for my keys. I knew where they were but was afraid that if I looked up at Duke, I'd have some sort of meltdown right there in his driveway.

"Something is up," said Duke. "You rushed over here bursting with news, and now you're not even going to tell me what it is?"

"It's hard to talk about." I took a deep breath. "But you're right. I owe you the truth. It's just, my dad and GiGi are fighting, and I think this might be it for them."

"That's all?" asked Duke.

"Isn't that enough?"

Duke glanced at me, skeptical. "Um, I know you got mad at me the last time I brought this up, but *Entertainment Weekly* did vote your dad 'Guy Most Likely to Have a Revolving Door Installed to His Bedroom' last year. So I don't really get why you're so surprised."

"I'm not surprised. I'm just upset."

"You don't even like GiGi."

"But I'm used to her. And the evil I know is better than the evil I don't know."

"You always say that."

"Because it's true." I opened up my car door.

"So, what's Austin's screenplay about?" Duke asked.

Panic welled up in my chest, and I felt my cheeks heat up. "Don't know," I said, probably too quickly.

"Aren't you curious?"

"Yeah. I have a copy. It's just . . . I haven't gotten to it yet."

"It's funny," he said.

"What?"

"I don't know." Duke shrugged. "Obviously, I didn't know him as well as you did, but I never really saw Austin as a writer. Yet supposedly this brilliant screenplay just appears out of nowhere. It's weird. Don't you think?"

"Yeah," I said with a nervous laugh. "I was pretty surprised too."

CHAPTER ELEVEN

Jess sobs as she drives away from UCLA. After a
few moments something dawns on her. Alex turned out
to be a cheater, which means she can legitimately
start dating his brother. Seeing the good in all
this, she begins to feel better. She pulls out her
cell and makes a call.

                              JESS
         Chad?

                              CHAD
         Hi, Jess.

                              JESS
         Guess what?

                              CHAD
         Aliens have invaded the Beverly Center.

                              JESS
         What?

CHAD

Wait. Don't tell me. You discovered a
new planet and you're naming it after
me. I just hope it's a real, old-school
planet and not one of those bullshit
balls of ice like Pluto.

JESS

What are you talking about?

CHAD

I don't know. You told me to guess.

JESS

Well, stop guessing. I'll just tell
you. It's over. Things with Alex are
really over this time.

CHAD

Really?

JESS

Yes, completely.

CHAD

That's great. What happened?

JESS

I'll tell you when I see you.

CHAD

Well, what did he say?

                              JESS
Nothing. I didn't give him a chance
to speak. That was the amazing thing
about it. I mean, at first it was a
shock, but now I realize this is for
the best.

                              CHAD
What is?

                              JESS
I sort of walked in on your brother
and Veronica. They were in bed and—

                              CHAD
Really?

                              JESS
Really. We're both cheating. So,
it's like I'm absolved of all guilt
in this mess. This will make things so
much easier.

                              CHAD
Are you sure you're okay?

                              JESS
I'm fine. Better than fine. This is a
huge relief. I'll be over in an hour,
okay? I just need to help Jake with a
paper first.

                              CHAD
Well, hurry up. I can't wait to see you.

                    JESS

Me too.

                    CHAD

And, Jess?

                    JESS

Yeah?

                    CHAD

Guess what.

                    JESS

Um, Starbucks is opening up a
franchise on Pluto?

                    CHAD

Close.

                    JESS

Then, what?

                    CHAD

I love you.

                    JESS

I love you, too.

Jess pulls into her driveway. She's beaming. She
runs into the house and starts yelling for her
brother.

                          JESS
             Jake? Where are you, Jake?

She goes to his room, but he's not there. She wanders
through the house and can't find him anywhere.
Finally, she heads outside. She sees Jake out by the
pool. There's a woman with him. She's rubbing his
shoulders with sunblock.

Jess smiles and starts to walk forward. Suddenly,
she stops.

As Jake turns around and kisses the woman, Jess gets
a better look at her. It's Ginger.

Her new stepmom and her brother are kissing.

Horrified, Jess runs back inside. They haven't seen
her.

Her cell phone rings. It's Chad.

                          CHAD
             Tell your brother you'll help him some
             other time. I can't wait!

                          JESS
             I, I have to go.

As Jess hangs up, tears spring to her eyes. She's
completely devastated.

Cut to: Jess, knocking on the door of an apartment
somewhere else in L.A.

Pilar opens the door and hugs Jess. (Pilar is Jess's former nanny. She's a tall, thin, beautiful Salvadoran woman with long, dark hair.)

PILAR
Jess! This is such a nice surprise.

JESS
I hope you don't mind my barging in like this.

PILAR
You're not barging in. You're always welcome here. I told you that when I left. I just don't know what took you so long.

JESS
You've only been here for a month.

PILAR
I know, but your brother is no stranger.

JESS
Really?

PILAR
Sure, I see him all the time. Just last week he helped me move these bookshelves in.

JESS
Jake knows how to move bookshelves?

PILAR

You're too hard on your brother, Jess.
I know he can be difficult at times,
but he means well, and he's got a good
heart. You know that.

JESS

Huh.

PILAR

Come in. Let me show you my new place.

Jess goes inside and looks around the one-bedroom
apartment.

JESS

It's so nice.

Pilar opens the closet door and walks in and out.

PILAR

Check out this closet. It's a walk-in.
I can't believe I have my own walk-in
closet in my own apartment in Santa
Monica.

JESS

It's great.

PILAR

Try it.

Jess walks in and out of the closet.

                          JESS

    It works.

They both laugh.

                          JESS

    The light is so great, you could get
    a sunburn in your living room.

                          PILAR

    I know. It's a good thing too. The
    beach is only five minutes away, but
    I hardly have time to go anymore. Work
    has been crazy-busy. I was there all
    morning.

                          JESS

    Work on a Saturday?

                          PILAR

    Yes, but it's okay because I love it.

They sit down in the living room.

                          PILAR

    So tell me everything. How's school?
    And Luke? Are your father and brother
    doing okay without me? Is Ginger
    behaving?

                          JESS

    It's funny you should mention Ginger.
    Um, this is kind of hard to say, but,
    well, you're the only person I could

tell this to. I just saw—

The phone rings, interrupting Jess.
Pilar jumps up.

                         PILAR
          I need to get that. Sorry, Jess. Hello?

Jess watches Pilar, who is speaking a steady stream
of Spanish into the phone. As time passes, her voice
becomes more animated and excited until she's
jumping up and down.

She hangs up the phone, looking thrilled.

                         JESS
          Good news?

                         PILAR
          Amazing news. I told you that Rosa, my
          little sister in El Salvador, is
          pregnant, right?

                         JESS
          Yes, I remember.

                         PILAR
          Well, she just found out she's having
          twins!

                         JESS
          That's amazing. Congratulate her for
          me.

PILAR

I will. I need to call her. That was
just my mom. She says hello, and she
wants to know if you got the sandals
she sent.

JESS

Sandals?

PILAR

They're chocolate-brown leather.

JESS

I don't think so.

PILAR

Hang on a second?

Jess nods, and sits back as Pilar makes another
call. As time passes, Jess gets sadder and sadder.
She realizes that she can't tell Pilar about her
family's problems. Pilar is so happy and things are
going so well for her. It wouldn't be fair to burden
her with the Brown family dysfunction. She doesn't
work for them anymore.

When Pilar finally gets off the phone, she turns
to Jess.

PILAR

She's due in two months, which is great
timing for me, because I should finally
be able to take some vacation time at
Christmas.

                         JESS
          That's great.

                         PILAR
          Oh, but here I am, going on and on
          about myself. What's new with you?

                         JESS
          Nothing. Things are good. Great,
          actually.

                         PILAR
          I'm so glad.

Jess stands up.

                         JESS
          It was so nice seeing you, Pilar.

                         PILAR
          It's wonderful seeing you. Thank you
          for coming over. Give your dad and Jake
          big hugs for me, okay?

                         JESS
          Sure thing.

                         PILAR
          It was so silly of me to worry. You're
          doing so well without me. All of you
          are!

Jess laughs nervously.

CHAPTER TWELVE

REREADING THOSE SCENES WAS LIKE RELIVING THE moment. Even now, three months later, I still felt the cold, raw shock of it.

I wish I could have explained how devastating it had been, seeing Jett and GiGi making out by the pool. I'd always known that my family was screwed up. But it wasn't until that moment that I realized I was just as bad. Worse, even, because I'd taken things even further. Cheating on Austin with his brother put me in the same category as GiGi. It was the last place I wanted to be.

Yet who could I have possibly explained that to? By the time I found out about the affair, Lubna was already up at school. (Plus, technically, she and my brother were back together. The two of them had spent the previous weekend up in Berkeley, where he'd apparently professed his undying devotion. She was so thrilled they were a couple again. This news would have crushed her.)

Duke was out. Our friendship seemed too new. Plus, whenever he made cracks about my dad, it bugged me and I didn't want to give him fresh material.

That left Carmen. But when I tried to tell her, I couldn't. Being in her cool Santa Monica apartment, seeing her so happy,

I realized that it wouldn't have been fair, burdening her with the mess when she had this great new life.

If only I'd confronted Jett when I found out. Or I could have told my father the truth. Sure, it would have been painful, but at least he'd have been able to deal with it in private.

I should have told someone, but instead, I wrote it all down. And now, this . . .

After fleeing Duke's, I couldn't face anyone at home, so I spent the rest of the day racking up charges on my credit card, thinking that shopping might make me feel better. But actually, it made me more depressed.

Since it was just four days before Christmas, the stores were crowded with people buying last-minute gifts. My family doesn't exchange gifts. Since Dad has no interests apart from work and infidelity, there's nothing Jett or I could ever get for him. And he doesn't have time to shop for us. It would be pointless, anyway, he explained years ago, since we have credit cards and he doesn't care what we buy, year round. I know I'm lucky, and complaining makes me sound incredibly spoiled. I'm not even complaining, exactly. I just can't help but wonder what it would be like to have a parent who knew what I was into and liked getting me things. Like this mom at Nordstrom who was raving to this saleslady about a cute purple dress that her daughter was just going to love.

Anyway, I'm just saying . . . I had to keep my mind off things. I came home late that night, went to bed, and slept late.

Most of Tuesday was filled with party preparations. I hadn't been lying to Duke. There was a lot of stuff to take care of. The guest list for this year's party was three times longer than usual. GiGi's doing—it was her first time playing hostess, and she wanted to go all out. Of course, to her this meant inviting the entire "A-list," as she called it, and then spending all week shopping, tanning, working out, and visiting her plastic surgeon for her fill of BOTOX and Restylane injections. That left me to deal with the logistics, and I was happy to have the distraction. Dealing with the caterer, florist, party planner, liquor store, etc., was almost enough to make me forget about the mess of my life.

At least it was enough until Tuesday night, when I overheard my dad saying something about finding a director for *Cold-Blooded*. Just *Cold-Blooded*. The movie already had a nickname, which meant people were talking about it. A lot. So much so that they couldn't even be bothered to call it by its full name. Things were happening. I'd been completely ignoring the problem, and all the while, stuff was moving forward.

I tossed and turned and hardly slept that night. On Wednesday morning I woke up in a panic, finally realizing that I had to do something.

I needed Carmen. Yes, she had her own life, but this was an emergency. Hoping that she might check her voice mail, I left her long and rambling messages at both her home and office, begging her to call me back. I even tried tracking her down in El Salvador but couldn't manage to find her family's number. It turns out Carmen's last name, Barraza, is as common in her native country as Jones is in the United States.

Things probably would have gone more smoothly if I were capable of speaking more than five words of Spanish. The decision I made in the eighth grade to take French instead has never felt more frivolous. I only signed up because I thought it would be cool to one day go to the Cannes Film Festival with my dad and impress him by ordering *un verre de l'eau et un sandwich de jambon*. It's ridiculous, I know. Dad has never once invited me to come with him. Plus, I've heard you can order a glass of water and a ham sandwich in English in any restaurant on the French Riviera and they'll know what you're talking about.

French waiters only pretend not to understand because they want you to feel bad about yourself, but in the end, you will get what you asked for, because they know Americans tip better than Europeans.

Jett got to go to the film festival in France two summers ago. Dad took him as a reward for actually finishing high school, but there was some incident with the girlfriend of an Italian director, which resulted in EggBrite losing a big picture and Jett coming home with a broken nose. No one told me the details, but suffice to say, I will not be showing off my French language skills in Europe anytime soon.

Duke speaks Spanish fluently, and under normal circumstances I'd have asked for his help, but I was avoiding him for the obvious reasons. Meanwhile, he'd been calling and texting me ever since I fled his trailer on Monday. I knew he was confused by my strange behavior. I wish I'd been able to think up a better excuse at the time, but more than that, I wish I could face him.

My life was in such shambles; I was actually looking forward to going back to school. Sure, I had more enemies there than Mussolini did in wartime Italy, but at least I'd be able to occupy my time calculating moles of various gasses at standard temperature and pressure, and slogging through Edith Wharton and Graham Greene novels. Tasks that were time consuming, if not exactly fascinating. Another plus? With schoolwork there was always a clear-cut way of doing things, a right and a wrong answer. My own twisted family drama? It was more like one of those *Choose Your Own Adventure* books, with all paths leading toward imminent disaster.

The eleven remaining days of winter break seemed interminable. I was dreading our trip to Ixtapa most of all. We were supposed to leave that Friday, Christmas morning, in two days. In my regular life it was easy to avoid my family, hang out with

Duke 24/7, and pretend like everything was just fabulous. Vacation was different. The rules would change. We were going to be stuck together at the same small hotel—maybe in adjoining rooms. I just can't imagine swimming, lounging around on the beach, and drinking virgin margaritas knowing all the while that my stepmom and my brother's girlfriend are one and the same. That pretty soon—thanks to me—everyone in town is going to know too.

And if all that weren't bad enough, I still had to get through the party. Just what I needed when I was on the verge of a nervous breakdown—to smile and pretend to be a happy and carefree high school junior in front of one hundred friends and business associates of my father. (Plus the extra two hundred people GiGi decided to invite.)

But that's exactly what I had to do. I owed it to my dad to hold it together. To pretend like everything was normal while that was still possible.

So on Wednesday night, I took a shower and then put on my favorite red strapless dress. Somehow, my hair turned out decent. It hung long and straight and shiny down my back. It was as if all the individual strands felt sorry for me and got together and decided that, for once, they should behave. Not much of a consolation prize, but it was something.

I was just finishing my makeup when I heard the doorbell. Figuring that someone else would get it, I ignored it. But no one did, and it kept on ringing.

Checking my clock, I saw that it was exactly eight o'clock. The party had been called for eight. I couldn't imagine who would actually show up on time.

After checking to make sure that my teeth were lipstick-free, I ran downstairs and flung open the door. My smile wavered when I found myself face-to-face with the Drs. Cooper.

"Hello, Jasmine," said Lori as she leaned over to give me a hug. Her vanilla-scented perfume made my nose twitch.

"Hi, Lori. Dr. Cooper. Please come in."

Dr. Cooper gave me an awkward kiss on the cheek and said, "I hope we're not too early."

"Not at all," I said. "You're right on time," which was true, at least technically.

As I wiped my eyes I realized that it wasn't Lori's perfume that was bothering me. This time last year, all four Coopers came to our party together. Seeing the two of them in the doorway, looking meek and incomplete, it struck me that Austin was gone and they'd never be the same. None of us would.

Taking a deep breath, I blinked back the tears, not convinced I could take the pressure for much longer. I felt like an overfilled tire—strong and sturdy looking from the outside, but bursting at the seams and on the verge of exploding.

"It's nice to see you again. Sunday's service was lovely," I said, and then immediately regretted it. That probably wasn't the type of thing you were supposed to say. But I wasn't really up on my memorial service etiquette. The only other one I'd ever been to was for my mom, and I was only two, so it's not like I can even remember being there. I just know that I was from the pictures.

One of the waiters hurried over to take our drinks order. Then we headed into the living room, where we sat down on opposite couches and grinned at one another silently—like seventh-graders at their first school dance.

The doorbell rang again, and I heard my dad greeting people in the entryway.

When Austin and I were a couple, the Coopers had me over for dinner all the time, and at first I never knew what to say or how to act. They were such a nice, normal family, the kind I'd only before seen on TV. It made my skin crawl. Back then, Lori always made polite conversation with me about school and whatever, and eventually she got me to relax. She was so nice that sometimes I pretended I was the Coopers' actual daughter rather than the girlfriend of one or both of their sons.

"We finally signed our deal with EggBrite," Dr. Cooper said.

"So I heard." I'd assumed it would happen after reading Monday's article, and Dad had confirmed it this morning before he left for work. "That's good news," I continued. "I just wish Austin were around to hear it."

Dr. Cooper pulled a tight-lipped smile and glanced at Lori, who looked at me for the first time that night. "I'm glad you brought him up," she said. "Because we need to talk to you about something. The screenplay went for a lot of money, as you probably know."

I nodded stupidly, realizing that, actually, I didn't know what a lot of money translated into. It probably wasn't appropriate to ask, but I was so curious. I couldn't help it. "Um, what did the screenplay go for?"

"One point two million dollars," Dr. Cooper said.

I took a sip of water to hide my shock. Wow, that was a lot of cash. Enough to bribe GiGi to flee the country with, or better yet, to leave town myself. I knew it was wrong to marvel about the money, but I couldn't help it. In a roundabout, messed-up way, I'd sort of earned it. If I hadn't co-opted the family's life for my material, my dad would have been so proud.

"We want to use the money in a way that honors Austin's memory," Lori said. "We're going to start a foundation in his name, and we'd like for you to be a part of it. Jett, too—we want all of his close friends involved."

Dr. Cooper stared into his gin and tonic, swirling it so that the ice clinked against the glass. "We're going to give out scholarships. At least one every year to a student who plans on studying medicine at UCLA."

It was nice that some good would come out of this whole mess. Although strange that they chose to create a scholarship for premed students, when studying science had made Austin miserable. Not that I could ever say this to his parents.

Instead, I told them, "Of course, I'd be honored to be a part of it." Then I shifted in my seat, smoothed my dress over my knees, and wondered how long I had to sit there. Because it was torture, pretending like everything was okay. Like I wasn't sitting on top of this humongous awful secret that would embarrass us all.

"Good." Dr. Cooper nodded once, perfunctorily. "We'll meet right after the New Year. By then, Lori will be back from Australia."

"You're going to Australia?" I asked.

"Yes, I thought it would be easier for Charlie if I went with him, to help him get settled there," she explained.

"Wait, what?"

Lori blinked at me. "Charlie is spending the semester in Sydney. I'm surprised he hasn't told you."

"No," I cried, unable, at the moment, to formulate another word. My stupor was probably raising suspicion, but it wasn't something I had any control over.

Luckily GiGi chose that moment to sweep in, all smiles and air kisses and apologies for having to miss the service on Sunday.

It was a welcome distraction for us all. She was my superhero for the moment—my adulterous superhero stepmom, dazzling one and all with her stunning emerald green gown, and her devastatingly gorgeous white-blond hair, which was piled up around her shoulders, in loose and chunky curls.

If it wasn't obvious to me that her messy-casual look took hours to create, all I had to do was glance at Raul, her hairdresser-makeup artist. He was slouched in the corner, sweating as he knocked back his drink. The poor guy had arrived at noon and he must have just finished.

I slipped away from the Coopers and wandered through the crowd. Jett was in one corner, talking to the actress who'd made the cover of *Vanity Fair* last month. My dad was nearby, catching up with Mary Beth and her new girlfriend.

Mary Beth directs those art house films, where nothing much happens in terms of plot but everyone feels alienated and they deal with it by smoking and talking and sipping red wine at fancy restaurants.

Normally, I'd have gone over to say hello, since Mary Beth was my favorite of Dad's ex-wives. They got married when I was seven and were together for two whole years. After their divorce, she still made a big effort to stay in touch, even though she'd moved to New York after their split. But tonight I felt too guilty to interact with anyone I knew. So I waved and kept my distance. This wasn't hard to do, because by now the party had swelled to the size where it was easy to disappear.

Sipping sparkling water, I had a series of nonsparkling conversations.

People asked me: "How's school? What's your favorite subject? Are you going away for Christmas? Where did you get that fabulous dress? And where are you applying to college?"

I answered as if on autopilot: "Fine. History. Yes, to Ixtapa. Some boutique in Malibu. Nowhere, I'm a junior."

"But you must have an idea," one woman pressed. She was wearing a tiny black dress with red platform heels, and her hair was pulled into low pigtails. In trying to look younger, she'd achieved the look of someone who was old and trying too hard.

"Where did you go to college?" I wanted to ask, her but didn't because that would have been rude.

It's not like I didn't know what she was doing. Ever since Jett got arrested for streaking naked across the stage at a U2 concert, lots of people have been trying to figure out if I'm a screwup too.

Where I plan on applying to college is a good benchmark for those curious about my performance level. If I was looking at the UCs and Stanford and perhaps some Ivies back east, I exceeded expectations. If I mentioned state schools and lesser-known colleges, or nothing at all, then they wouldn't be surprised.

Most people were at least subtle about it. This woman wouldn't let up.

I could have told her that the admissions people at Amherst had asked me to apply early, or I could have pulled a Gwyneth Paltrow, telling her I wasn't sure that college was for me at all. But both would have been lies, and I wasn't in the mood to prove anything.

"Somewhere far away from here," I replied finally, smiling and turning to leave.

The house was packed with people, and it was way too loud.

The conversations that went on around me competed with the ones I was having with myself, in my head.

Walking into the dining room, I heard someone say, "GiGi looks beautiful."

I thought, *If only she could act.*

As I headed out to the patio by the pool, someone else said, "GiGi and Marvin are a magnificent couple."

I thought, *Too bad she's sleeping with his son.*

When I went back inside, passing through the living room, I overheard a woman whisper, "Jasmine looks just like her mom. It's such a shame she never knew her."

This time I felt like turning around and shouting, "Shut up. Who the hell are you? And why do you think you can just say that?"

But I moved on, clutching my drink so tightly, I'm surprised the glass didn't shatter in my hand. It's frustrating—the way so many people think they know my mom. To them, she's merely an icon, this image made up of a collection of pictures and interviews. Since I don't have any real memories of her, that's all I have too. It feels crappy, and on another level it's also infuriating that I have to share her with the world.

Charlie was someone I could talk to about that.

He knew things that no one else did. I told him about the box I kept under my bed—the one filled with copies of my mom's old interviews and DVDs of every movie she ever appeared in. How when I was feeling down or empty, I'd hole up in my room and pore over her words. Sometimes I'd stay up all night and watch five of her movies in a row. Always searching for something more, something new or different that I'd somehow missed before, and usually coming up disappointed. Sometimes I liked to bring myself to tears over it. He didn't think I was pathetic for that.

Before we started dating, when he was just my SAT tutor/friend, I told him about that. And a few days later he gave me a silver necklace molded into the shape of a DNA strand. A weird gift that I didn't understand until he explained. It was a reminder, he said, that I knew my mom better than most people. That she was more than a public image to me, even if I couldn't remember her. I didn't need to recall specific details because she's actually a part of me.

The problem with this logic, I now realized, was that my dad was a part of me too. The lying-and-cheating part.

Which brought me back to Charlie. I'd tried apologizing to him so many times, but he wouldn't listen—not before or even after his brother died.

It didn't make sense that the guy who understood what he'd understood, and knew how to say the exact right thing when I needed him to, would move halfway around the world without even saying good-bye.

But thinking about Charlie made me realize something else. I owed him an explanation. This wasn't just about me and my family. He needed to know that he was in the screenplay. That Austin was a big part of it too. Maybe he'd warn his parents. None of us wanted them to be humiliated when the truth got out. And I certainly couldn't tell them.

I don't know why this hadn't occurred to me before. Charlie's leaving in the morning just made things that much more urgent.

Grabbing my coat, I headed out the front door and got into my car.

I only started to lose my nerve on the drive over to Charlie's house, because our breakup scene was replaying in my head.

I pictured it so clearly. As if it already *were* the movie it was on the verge of becoming.

CHAPTER THIRTEEN

With no one to turn to, Jess becomes paralyzed by the news of her brother and stepmother's affair. Over the next few days she lingers around the house in a zombie-like state, unable to go to school or to speak with anyone.

As time goes by, Luke, Alex, and Chad all call, but Jess can't bring herself to speak with any of them. She does listen to the messages they leave on her cell phone:

> (V.O.) ALEX
> Jess, I'm sorry you had to see that. I mean, I'm sorry it happened. But that was the first time with Veronica, I swear. And we were drunk and I was stupid, and it will never, ever happen again.

> (V.O.) CHAD
> Jess, where are you? Please tell me what's going on.

(V.O.) LUKE
You must call me. Not only did Mr.
Blunt write back, he also sent a
picture from fantasy pro-football
camp. Did you know that he used to have
a mullet? That is so typical. So, how
was Operation Dump Alex? I want all the
gory details. Call me.

Cut to:

Jess in sweatpants, unshowered, hair a mess, staring
at the television, eating Reese's peanut butter cups
straight from a jumbo bag.

We hear her voice mail messages in the
background. . . .

LUKE
Okay, maybe I was a little insensitive
the other day, so I'm sorry. I'm sure
it was hard, but what's up with
ditching school? Are you sick? Or do
you have someplace better to be? And if
you have someplace better to be, how
come I wasn't invited?

CHAD
I'm guessing you're upset about my
brother, and I just wanted to let you
know that I understand. But remember,
you were going over there to break up
with him. And if you're not ready, if
you need some space, that's cool. I can

wait. Just call me back and tell me
that, okay?

                    ALEX
Please, let me explain. The thing with
Veronica means nothing to me. And it
wasn't even good. Well, it wasn't
great. . . .

Cut to:

Jess has sunk into such an agonizing pit of
despair that she's watching the E! channel. An
image of her father and Ginger, walking down a
red carpet on their way to a movie premiere,
flashes on the screen. Jess starts throwing mini-
Reese's at the screen. She's really losing it.

Finally Jess pulls out of her funk. We see her making
a call and asking someone to come over at noon on
Saturday.

Cut to:

Interior of the Browns' house. Someone is knocking
on the door. Jess peeks through the window and sees
Chad. She sighs. It's obvious she's dreading this.
Still, she has no choice. She has to get through
this, so she opens the door.

                    JESS
        Sorry I didn't call sooner.

                              CHAD
              It's been three days, Jess. You can't
              imagine what I've been thinking. And
              you were so cryptic on the phone.
              What's up with that?

                              JESS
              I know. I'm sorry. It's been hard for
              me, too. Believe me.

Jess looks past Chad to her driveway. Alex is
pulling up.

                              JESS
              Shit.

Chad turns around. Sees the car.

                              CHAD
              Don't worry. We'll just tell him I'm
              here to tutor you.

                              JESS
              Promise me you won't hate me for what
              I'm about to do.

                              CHAD
              What do you mean?

                              JESS
              Just promise me.

Alex is getting out of his car. Chad speaks in a
whisper.

CHAD

I can't believe he had to show up now.

JESS

I invited him.

CHAD

Why would you invite him here if you
invited me?

JESS

I've been thinking about things, and I
can't be that person, you know? I can't
be like them. Like her.

CHAD

Like who?

JESS

Like Ginger.

CHAD

You sound nothing like Minnie Mouse,
and your boobs are totally real. You
couldn't be like Ginger if you tried.

JESS

That's not what I meant. I can't
explain it. Just, please don't hate
me. This is something I have to do.

Alex comes to the front door. He's holding flowers.
Jess looks at them. He blushes. They both realize

this is a feeble gesture, even more embarrassing
in front of Chad. Alex tosses the flowers over
his shoulder.

ALEX
Forget you even saw that.

(He turns to Chad)

Hey, what are you doing here?

CHAD
I was about to ask you the same thing.

ALEX (TO JESS)
I thought you already aced your SATs.

JESS
Alex, we need to break up.

ALEX
Okay, I figured that was coming, but
why the audience?

JESS
I'm not breaking up with you for
cheating on me with Veronica. I
deserved that and I need to be honest
with you, now. The thing is, I've been
cheating on you, too.

ALEX
What?

JESS
I'm sorry, Alex. It was horrible of me.
I guess we're both really screwed up.
Or maybe we're not and this is just what
happens. Maybe we broke up a while ago,
but just didn't have the conversation.
Because we both know that things have
been weird for a while.

ALEX
You cheated on me?

JESS
Yes, and I feel terrible about it. You
know what it's like, so you have to
understand. . . .

ALEX
That's bullshit. Who is he?

No one says anything. Jess looks at Chad and mouths
an apology. Eventually it dawns on Alex.

ALEX
You've got to be fucking kidding me.

JESS
We never meant to hurt you.

CHAD (BACKING UP)
I'm sorry, Alex.

Alex shoves Chad, who falls to the ground. They get
in a wrestling match on the front lawn. Chad manages

to pin Alex, but only briefly. Soon Alex overpowers
him and starts punching him in the stomach.

                    JESS
        Stop it!

Jess gets into the fray, jumping on Alex's back. The
three of them are wrestling. It's a big mess, until
someone turns on the sprinklers. Everyone is stunned
enough to stop and look up to see who did this. It's
Jake.

                    JAKE
        What the hell is going on here?

Everyone looks up at him, but no one answers.
Alex storms off.
Later, inside the house, Chad is sitting in the
kitchen with Jess.

He's soaking wet and is icing his eye.

                    CHAD
        Well, that went well.

                    JESS
        I'm sorry.

                    CHAD
        It's okay. I'll heal. And you're worth
        the pain. I'm glad we don't have to
        sneak around anymore.

                    JESS
        Chad, we can't be together.

CHAD

Very funny.

JESS

I'm serious. I don't deserve you.
Right now I don't deserve anyone.

CHAD

You're not actually dumping both of us.

JESS

It's the only thing I can do.

CHAD

What? No, wait. That is so screwed up.

JESS

I know, and I wish there were another way.

CHAD (ANGRY)

Did you arrange this so you'd save
time? Break up with both of your
boyfriends at once?

JESS

Don't be mean.

CHAD

It's amazing that you can sit there and
tell me not to be mean.

Chad walks out the door. Jess stays seated in the
kitchen. When she hears the front door slam, she
bursts into tears.

Jake walks into the kitchen, but Jess's back is to
him. He heads into the pantry.

                         JAKE
     I don't believe this!

                    JESS (SNIFFING)
     What?

                         JAKE
     We're out of Lucky Charms.

Jess leaves the room.

Cut to: The next day, Jess and Luke lunch at an
outdoor café.

                         LUKE
     But why did you have to break up with
     both of them?

                         JESS
     I can't explain it.

                         LUKE
     You're crazy about Chad. I don't get
     why you're denying yourself this.

                         JESS
     He's so good and nice. I don't deserve
     him. He's better off staying away from
     my whole family, actually.

                    LUKE
Okay, where is this coming from?

                    JESS
Do you think infidelity can be passed
down? Like it's a gene or something?

                    LUKE
I'm not going there.

                    JESS
Come on. I really want to know what you
think.

            LUKE (SHAKING HIS HEAD)
The last time I made a crack about your
dad's cheating, you wouldn't talk to
me for a week.

                    JESS
That's because you were quoting
something you read in *Entertainment
Weekly*.

                    LUKE
Still, you have to admit, it's a touchy
subject.

                    JESS
Okay, yes. I'm sensitive about it. But
maybe I have a good reason to be. Think
about it: My dad cheats on almost
everyone. Jake is cheating on Lucy.

                              LUKE
          He's cheating on her again? With who?

                              JESS
          I don't know.

                              LUKE
          So you just assume?

                              JESS
          No, trust me, it's true. But that's
          not my point. It's just, here I am,
          cheating on my boyfriend. With his
          brother. Am I any better?

                              LUKE
          It's different with you.

                              JESS
          How so?

                              LUKE
          You fell in love with Chad.

                              JESS
          Maybe my dad falls in love every other
          month too. Maybe I'm just genetically
          wired to have a messed-up love life.

                              LUKE
          I don't think it works that way.

Suddenly Jess sees Alex walk into the restaurant,
and hides behind a menu.

                    JESS
    Oh, no!

                    LUKE
    What are you doing?

Jess shushes him, but it's too late. Alex sees Luke
and goes over to say hi. Jess peeks out from behind
the menu, sheepish.

                    JESS
    Hey, Alex.

                    ALEX
    Can we talk?

                    JESS
    There's nothing to talk about.

                    ALEX
    Please?

                    JESS
    We're kind of busy here.

                    ALEX
    Well, can I see you later? Come by the
    dorm. I have all your stuff and it's
    just sitting in the corner, which is
    depressing me.

                    JESS
    So give it to Veronica.

                              ALEX
          She's not even your size. Your leather
          jacket was swimming on her.

Jess glares at Alex.

                              ALEX
          Not that she tried it on. Look, just
          please come by later so we can talk.

                              JESS
          Fine.

As Alex walks away, Luke shakes his head.

                              JESS
          What?

                              LUKE
          Talking and going to pick up your stuff
          is just an excuse to have one last hookup.

                              JESS
          It is not.

                              LUKE
          How much you want to bet you hook up
          with him?

                              JESS
          I will not hook up with him.

                              LUKE
          Fifty bucks.

                    JESS
    Fine, it'll be the easiest money I
    ever made.

Cut to: Alex's dorm room. Jess and Alex are hooking up.

Cut to: School the next day. Jess is handing Luke
some cash. Later that same day, she runs into Chad in
the hall.

                    CHAD
    Can we talk?

Cut to: Behind the gym. Jess and Chad making out.
Cut to: Jess's bedroom. Jess and Alex are making out.
Chad drives by and sees Alex's car. Gets upset.
Cut to: Later that night, at Jess's front door.
Horrible fight between Jess and Chad.

                    CHAD
    You're still seeing him?

                    JESS
    No. I'm not.

                    CHAD
    I saw his car here.

                    JESS
    It was a mistake. Last week he asked me
    to stop by and pick up my stuff, and we
    got to talking. . . . I never thought
    anything would happen.

                              CHAD
Bullshit. Everyone knows that's the
oldest excuse for one last hookup!

                              JESS
Okay, how come everyone knows that but
me?

                              CHAD
You're not over my brother.

                              JESS
He was my first boyfriend. I'm sorry,
but this is all harder than I thought
it would be.

                              CHAD
Well, let me make things easier for
you. I'm out of here.

                              JESS
Wait!

                              CHAD
I tried waiting, and that didn't work.
You can't have us both, and now there's
really no excuse for what you're doing.
Maybe this is exciting for you and maybe
it's fun in a sick way. Maybe you did
this all to get back at my brother
forbeing such an asshole, and if that's
the case, I won't be a part of it.

                              JESS
Please don't go.

CHAD

I actually felt bad about the way my
brother treated you, but I guess you
two deserve each other.

JESS

I'm sorry.

CHAD

Stop saying that. Don't be sorry. Just
don't ever call me again.

CHAPTER FOURTEEN

TURNS OUT CHARLIE WAS MUCH BETTER AT STICKING
to his convictions than I was. That was the last thing he ever said
to me. I wish he'd have let me explain why I'd had to end things,
but he never gave me the chance.

Not that I blamed him. I didn't deserve his forgiveness.

Anyway, that's not why I drove to the Coopers' house so suddenly.

I was there because this was my last chance. I needed to tell
Charlie the truth about the screenplay.

Taking a deep breath, I headed to the front door and rang
their bell.

When Charlie answered, he didn't seem surprised to see me.
Of course, he didn't seem all that happy, either.

"Hey," he half grunted.

"Hey, yourself." It used to be that Charlie's eyes lit up when
he saw me. I know it wasn't fair to expect that now, and I didn't.
But I did ache for it.

Yet tonight he wasn't even letting me inside. He leaned
against the door frame, arms crossed over his chest, stiff and
tense. His hair had grown, and his bangs were hanging over the
top of his glasses.

"What do you want?" he asked coldly.

Simple question. Complicated answer.

I wanted everything to be different. For Austin to be alive. I wanted to have noticed Charlie for who he was two years ago, to not have seen Jett and GiGi. And to never have written about their affair.

What I wanted was too many things I could never have.

"What are you doing here?" he asked.

"I just heard about Australia, and . . ." I tried to meet his gaze, but he wouldn't look at me.

Instead, he put his hands in his pockets and stared at the ground. "You knew I was looking into that exchange program last fall."

"You said you didn't think you wanted to go. And isn't it summer there right now?"

"My mom has some cousins I can stay with in Sydney, so I'm going early."

"Because of me?"

I saw a flash of annoyance in his eyes. He stood up straight and finally met my gaze. "Contrary to what you might think, Jasmine, not everything is about you."

My stomach turned. "I didn't mean it like that. I know that came out wrong. It's just . . . I don't know, Charlie. I'm just so sorry about Austin. About everything, really. You deserved better. Both of you did."

"I know, and you've already said this."

Obviously, I was the last person Charlie wanted to deal with. But I'd shown up on his doorstep for a reason. This was my only chance, and I was blowing it.

"Have you read *Cold-Blooded, Two-Timing Rat?*" I asked.

"No," he replied.

"Um, do you know what it's about? Because—"

"No offense, Jasmine, but I have a lot going on right now. I don't really care about Austin's screenplay. It's so messed up that people are making such a big deal out of the whole thing. I mean, who cares about some stupid movie when Austin is dead? My parents keep talking about his spirit, and what he'd want, and how great it is that his memory will live on, but it's bullshit. It's not like any of it's going to bring him back."

"Do you even know what it's about?"

"Aren't you listening to me?" asked Charlie. "I'm telling you I don't care."

"But it's more complicated, because actually—"

"Look," he said, interrupting. "I have a lot of packing to do. And shouldn't you be at your party right now?"

"When are you coming back?" I was stalling. I needed to tell him the truth, but didn't know where to begin.

"The semester is over in June, but I'll probably stay for the summer, too." He shrugged, like it didn't even matter, like he was going away for the weekend. "I'll see how it goes."

"I'll miss you," I said.

"Bye, Jasmine." He closed the door before I could say another word. He even locked it, as if I'd barge in if he didn't take necessary precautions.

I stood there on the doorstep, feeling like an idiot, wondering why I was so convinced that Charlie would care. It didn't have to matter to him because when the truth came out, he'd be on the other side of the world.

Since I wasn't in any shape to go back to the party, I drove around for a while, and ended up on Coldwater Canyon. I took it all the way up to the top, stopping at Mulholland Drive, at the lookout point where Austin and I sometimes went. Since there weren't any other cars there, I took the narrow dirt path to the edge and turned off the engine. Sitting there at the top of the canyon, I could see all the tiny sparkling lights of the valley. It was impossible to see the entire west side. For that, you'd have to climb even higher. Austin once claimed it was the perfect metaphor for life in L.A. The thing is, I never could tell if he thought this was a good thing or a bad thing. And now I'd never know.

I don't know how long I stayed out there. Just that by the time I drove home, the party showed every sign of being over. Glasses of champagne stood half empty and defeated, liquid no longer bubbling with possibility. Couch cushions sat lumpy and askew. The caterers had turned into the cleanup crew, stacking chairs, clearing plates, and sweeping crumbs off the floor. Wiping away any and all evidence of festivities, they were brisk and efficient, like they had better places to be.

I wish I did.

"Jasmine!" called my father. "There you are."

"Hey, Dad." I headed over to him, realizing that I hadn't talked to him all night. "Great party."

"Well, it would have been great if we hadn't run out of wine so early in the night." He seemed annoyed, almost like he was blaming me, and I didn't know why. "Where have you been, anyway?"

I was surprised he noticed I was gone. "I was out."

"Well, you were supposed to be here when the wine was delivered yesterday. I wish you'd told me it never came."

"But it did come," I said.

"Then why is the wine refrigerator filled with kombucha tea?" he asked. "Is this some sort of joke?"

"What? No. It's GiGi's. Kombucha tea is supposed to be stored at the same temperature and humidity as wine."

"So what?" asked my dad.

"So, GiGi cleared out the wine fridge to make room for her

supply. When the liquor guys showed up yesterday, I had them put everything in the hall closet instead."

"Well, why didn't you tell me or the caterers? Or even GiGi? She had no idea about this."

"I'm sorry. I didn't mean to be gone for so long. I'll show you where it is." I reached for his arm, but he stepped away from me.

"It's too late, Jasmine. The party's over."

Dad walked off, heading to the small crowd milling around by the back door. Now he was all smiles, laughing and cracking jokes as he ushered the remaining party guests from the main part of the house into the screening room.

It was so unfair that he was blaming this on me. It was his stupid party. I didn't even want to be here. And it was his awful wife and her ridiculous tea fetish that caused this problem in the first place. Although it's not like I could complain, because there were still plenty of people around.

Every year after the party, Dad invites a select number of guests to stay after to watch EggBrite's latest Christmas picture in our screening room. He makes a big deal out of it—as if it's everyone's greatest wish to see some blockbuster movie two whole days before it's released in regular theaters.

People do get into it, or at least they act as if they do. That's the unspoken rule. Regardless of how you truly feel about the movie, you have to pretend to love it. Or at least I do. I got in trouble when I was in the eighth grade because I really hated the film that year and I made the mistake of saying so in front of the director. Dad was so embarrassed, he grounded me for a week. I was only being honest, but I never made that mistake again.

I joined the crowd outside, shuffling past the pool to the screening room on the other side. It was then that I noticed Duke, standing alone and looking bored. I'd forgotten that I'd begged him to come and he was doing me a huge favor by showing up. Family cocktail parties were a drag. Now that Madonna had moved to England, there was never anyone good to talk to.

"Where have you been?" Duke asked.

I hurried over and kissed him on the cheek. "You look nice," I said, which doubled as the truth and my feeble attempt to smooth things over. "Sorry."

"You're sorry for what?" he asked. "Not returning my ten phone calls? Or for begging me to come to a party that you didn't even bother attending?"

"I was here earlier, I swear. I'm sorry, Duke. I just forgot."

"What's going on with you? You've been acting weird ever since I got back from New York."

At least I could tell him part of the truth. "Charlie is leaving for Australia tomorrow. He's going for the whole semester and he didn't even tell me. I just happened to find out because I was talking to his parents. So I went over to his house to say good-bye. Except it didn't go so well. And then I didn't feel like coming back, so I just drove around for a while."

I didn't mention that I'd spent the better part of the evening sitting in a parked car by myself. That would have made me sound too pathetic.

"So you've been driving around alone while I've been stuck here," said Duke.

"I forgot that you were coming."

"Is that supposed to make me feel better?" he asked.

"That came out wrong. I'm really sorry." I linked my arm through Duke's and pulled him toward the screening room. "Please forgive me, okay? Come on. We should hurry up and sit before all the good seats are gone."

"I'm not staying for the movie," said Duke.

"But we've hardly had a chance to talk."

"Not my fault." Duke shook his head. "I've spent enough time at your house tonight, not talking to you. I don't need to do so for two more hours in a dark theater. Plus, the movie is supposed to be lousy."

"Shh!" I raised a finger to my lips, which at least made him smile.

"You are loyal to a fault," he said.

"It's complicated."

Duke shrugged. "It always is with you, but fine, whatever. We don't have to get into this now. You know where I am. Call me if you want to, and if not, well, have fun in Ixtapa."

"How'd you know about Ixtapa?" I wondered.

"I overheard GiGi. She's been talking about it all night," said Duke. "Apparently you're staying at the only five-star hotel there."

"Fabulous. I can't wait," I mumbled.

"Well, when you get back, we really need to figure out a plan for the maps. The whole thing was your idea, anyway, and I'm not sacrificing my grade in economics for your secret little drama," Duke said.

I watched him disappear back into the house, knowing I should go after him, to apologize again, but my dad was standing by the door impatiently, motioning for me to hurry up and get my butt inside.

Why I felt any loyalty to him, after he'd just yelled at me for no good reason, I can't explain. Not to Duke, or to anyone.

The screening room was crowded. It's a good thing Duke didn't stay, because by the time I got in, there was only one open seat. It was in the corner of the back row, next to some guy, who was tall and thin. He had a beard and glasses, but I couldn't tell who he was until I stepped on his foot and heard his voice—in the form of a yelp. Only then did I realize I was dealing with one of my least favorite people in the world.

"Well, if it isn't my good friend Barry Wentworth," I said sarcastically. "I didn't realize I'd have the pleasure of finding you here."

"Your dad's standards have really sunk," Barry replied.

"Either that or the security is lax," I said as I sat down next to him.

Barry Wentworth calls himself a freelance journalist and photographer. I call him a hack who spends his life stalking stars and digging for dirt with the hopes of exposing secrets he can turn into profit. Barry is the worst kind of tabloid reporter.

He's really into Dumpster diving, which means he'll do things like dig through the Olsen twins' garbage can in search of diet pills. Once he chased Lindsay Lohan down Wilshire Boulevard, drove her off the road, took pictures of her and the wreck, and then wrote a story chronicling her hazardous driving. He's the guy who crashed my sixteenth birthday party, snuck in a camera, and then sold the pictures to *People* magazine. I'm just the daughter, so he didn't care about me, of course. Just about the over-the-top party and the A-list guests that my dad's girlfriend had invited. Still, I was the one who had to deal with the consequences. People like him don't ever think about how their work can really hurt people. Or if they do, they certainly don't care, which is even worse.

In the screenplay version of my life, I call Barry Wentworth's character Barry Wentworth. That's right, I figured that a guy who spends his entire life exploiting celebrities for profit doesn't deserve to have his privacy kept. Using Barry's real name was the one thing I didn't regret in this whole big mess. And if anyone in the business recognized his name, I'm sure they'd get a kick out of it too.

"I'm sorry about your boyfriend," Barry said.

My shoulders tensed. I didn't trust this guy, nor did I understand what he was getting at. My thoughts immediately went to

Charlie. Had Barry followed me to the Coopers' house? Had he witnessed my humiliation? Why would he even care? "What are you talking about?" I asked.

"I wrote the piece for the *L.A. Times* about Austin Cooper's screenplay," said Barry. "Your name came up in the research, of course. I would've called, but I figured I'm the last person you'd want to hear from, especially about this."

"You don't really think I'd buy that you're that sensitive, do you?"

"Okay, true," said Barry. "I knew it would be a waste of a phone call because you'd refuse to speak to me, as usual."

"So you interviewed Violet instead?"

"Obviously. She was much more civil than you'd have been."

"Only because she doesn't know any better," I replied. Yes, I sounded smug but I couldn't help myself. Barry brought out the worst in me.

"You and Austin went out for over a year," said Barry. "Isn't that right?"

"Don't you have anything better to do than to track the romantic lives of teenagers?" I asked.

"It's not like I'm doing this for my health, Jasmine. It's my job, and for your information, I'm a very good journalist."

"Can tabloid reporters actually be called journalists? It seems so wrong that someone like you should fall into the same category as Woodward and Bernstein."

Barry laughed. "Trust me, Jasmine. This is not all the writing I do."

"What, you're working on a screenplay, too?" I threw out.

"Why, yes, how did you know?" Barry asked, for once seeming genuinely surprised.

"Everyone in this city is working on a screenplay," I said, not exactly impressed.

"Even you?" asked Barry.

Ouch. Before I could answer him, the lights went out and the movie began.

I turned my attention to the costume drama on the screen. EggBrite's latest picture was called *The Wizard, Romeo.* Its Shakespeare meets Harry Potter, in a world where the star-crossed lovers' families are in an ancient feud about magic. The Montagues are all wizards and witches, while the Capulets are mortal.

It was filmed in Budapest, which was supposed to pass for fifteenth-century Italy. Dad had spent a lot of time on location for the movie last year. I read somewhere that he'd been having an affair with the lead actress. If this was true, I don't think it lasted very long because I never met her. All I know is that it factored into his last breakup, pre-GiGi. Or maybe it was two breakups ago. It's too hard to keep track on my own.

Last year, Barry created a time line of my dad's love life and it got published in *Us Weekly.* Although I'd saved it because it turned out to be a handy reference, more accurate than my own memory, it's also incredibly depressing.

Of course, the fact that my love life is almost timeline–worthy makes things even worse.

I tried getting my mind off things by focusing on the movie, but it was hard. *The Wizard, Romeo* was so bad that the two hours seemed to stretch into four.

After the credits finished rolling, the lights went up. People talked about the wonderful writing and the vivid scenery and all of the amazing performances.

"Mirabella is going to be huge. She's sure to get a nod from the Oscar committee," said Janet, the publicity guru.

Sure, I thought. *If there was an award for best cleavage.*

"What I love is that the story is so unique," said some new

guy from marketing. "Wizards and witches. It's brilliant. No one is doing that these days."

Was he kidding? Or has he been living in a cave for the past ten years?

I looked around the room, panning the fake-cheerful faces in search of my brother. One of the few things we had in common was a disdain for all of the sucking up that went on after screenings. But Jett was nowhere to be found. I sort of resented that he'd been smart enough to sneak out.

Once they were finished fawning, Dad announced, "I hope you'll all join us here next year, when we'll be screening Austin Cooper's film, *Cold-Blooded, Two-Timing Rat.*"

As if I needed to be reminded. I stood up and headed toward the exit. Before I got outside, GiGi made her own announcement. "And if all goes well," she said, "I'll be starring in the movie, playing the part of Jessica Brown."

I let out a laugh, half in shock and half in outrage. How did GiGi think she was going to play me? She had to be kidding. I looked to my dad for an explanation, or at least a confirmation that she wasn't serious. He merely leveled his gaze at me as if to say, "Of course GiGi will be auditioning. Why are you so surprised?"

It was too much. I couldn't stop myself from saying, "There's no way GiGi can play Jess!"

And I guess I was pretty loud, because the next thing I knew, everyone in the room was staring at me.

CHAPTER FIFTEEN

CHALLENGING MY DAD'S WIFE IN A CROWDED screening room had the exact opposite effect of yelling "Fire!" in a packed movie theater. Rather than set off mass hysteria with people trampling all over one another in a desperate attempt to flee, I somehow managed to make everyone freeze in their footsteps and gape at me. It was so silent, I could almost hear the blood draining from my face.

This was bad. No one knew what to think. At least, I hoped they didn't. Dad glared at me. GiGi just seemed confused. Barry had this strange grin on his face, like he knew there was something going on. This was dangerous, so I did my best to try to smooth things over.

"I'm just kidding!" I said, forcing a laugh. "That's awesome news!" Walking up to GiGi, I gave her a hug. "It's about time you starred in a movie, and you'll make a great Jessica Green."

"Thanks," said GiGi. "But isn't it Jessica Brown?"

"What?" I asked.

"Jessica Brown," GiGi repeated. "That's the name of the lead character."

"Oh, right," I said. "Sorry about that. I'm, uh, still in the middle of it."

As everyone filed out of the room, I cursed myself for making such a huge mistake.

I hurried toward the exit, feeling Barry's prying eyes on me. Before I had the chance to tell him he was being creepy, GiGi pulled me aside and whispered, "My audition is right after we get back from Mexico. Maybe we can go over lines together on the trip. If you don't mind, that is. It would really help me out."

"Um, of course," I managed to croak out. "I'm happy to help."

"Good, that would mean so much to me," said GiGi.

I forced a yawn and stepped away. "Well, I'm pretty beat."

After saying my good-byes to the remaining guests, I fled to my bedroom and closed the door behind me. Flopping down onto my bed, I stared up at the ceiling.

This was getting crazy.

How could my stepmom play not just a seventeen-year-old girl, but one based on me? It was absurd, outrageous, and, most of all, insulting. For one thing, GiGi was twenty-three. But more important, she couldn't even act. Any role would be a stretch for her, but this one? It was impossible.

Yes, I realized that worrying about casting decisions was beside the point, but I couldn't help myself. This was just one more reason why I had to put a stop to this movie.

Obviously it was too late to tell my father the truth. He had too much invested.

I had to talk to Charlie again, to make him listen this time. Once he understood how serious this was, he'd warn his parents and they'd put a stop to it. Someone had to.

Sitting up, I pulled out my cell and tried calling him again, but he didn't answer. This didn't surprise me. He recognized my phone number and as I'd confirmed earlier in the evening, he had no interest in talking to me. I decided to try him from my dad's line, thinking that maybe if he saw a call from an unfamiliar extension, he'd actually answer. It was worth a shot, anyway.

I crept to the top of the steps and listened for conversation. Once I was sure that the guests were gone, I headed downstairs and opened up the door to my dad's office.

Then I screamed, because the room wasn't empty. Some random man was lurking behind his desk.

Startled, he looked up at me. It was Barry Wentworth. "Will you keep it down?" he asked.

"What are you still doing here?" I asked.

"Looking for the bathroom."

"There's one in the screening room."

"It was taken," said Barry.

"Well, there's no bathroom in here."

"I realize that now. I must have made a wrong turn. I was just leaving when you came in."

"No, you weren't." I glared at him. "You were snooping."

"I was not." Barry held up his empty hands, as if that proved anything.

"Whatever," I said. "Follow me." I led him to the nearest actual bathroom, in the hallway just off the kitchen.

As I waited for him outside, I couldn't help but overhear Dad and GiGi. They were arguing in the next room.

GiGi's voice was even more high-pitched than usual. "I know I wasn't supposed to say anything, but I couldn't help it. I'm just excited about the audition."

"You shouldn't have announced that in front of our guests. You know there are other people interested in that role. Established actresses. It's not just going to be yours automatically. I told you from the beginning that you're not going to get preferential treatment." My father sounded angry. Fed up.

"I know that!" GiGi yelled. "All I want is a chance, just like anyone else. I said if all goes well, I'll play Jess. I didn't say it was definite."

"Well, I wish you'd consider reading for another part. The stepmother, for instance."

"I'm far too young to play a stepmother!" GiGi shrieked.

Any irony in this situation was lost on both of them. Not that I could appreciate it at the moment either. Their voices were so loud, I was sure Barry was able to hear their conversation through the door. No wonder he was taking so long. I began to regret not sending him to the bathroom out back, by the screening room. Or better yet, I should have just made him leave the property.

"This role is very important to me," GiGi went on. "I understand Jess, and I know I can do this."

"You haven't even read the script!" my dad screamed.

"That's because your daughter has the only copy in the house."

Just then Barry opened up the door. As he cleaned his glasses with the bottom of his shirt, he looked at me with raised eyebrows. "Trouble in paradise?" he asked.

I laughed and played dumb. "I'm not sure what you're talking about," I said. "Let me walk you out."

The fastest way to the front door was through the kitchen, so I raised my voice to a near-shout, hoping that Dad and GiGi would keep it down. At least until this guy was off the property. "It's right this way, Barry."

As I steered him through, the two of them were all smiles.

Dad reached out his hand. "Lovely to see you, Barry. Thanks for coming by."

"It's my pleasure," said Barry. "It was a great party, and I loved *The Wizard, Romeo.*"

"Yes, good. Glad to hear it. We're expecting big returns on that one. Have a safe drive home."

"I will," said Barry. "Thanks again for inviting me. And good-bye, Jasmine. As always, it was lovely chatting with you."

"If by 'lovely' you mean 'nerve-grating and annoying,' then I agree with you completely," I replied as I walked him to the front door.

Before he left, Barry winked at me and I could hardly contain my look of disgust.

After closing the door behind him, I turned around to find my dad standing in the entryway.

"Jasmine, please don't be rude to our guests," Dad said.

"Why did you invite Barry, anyway?" I asked.

"I invited him," said GiGi, walking into the room. "I thought it would be nice if he wrote about the party."

"That's ridiculous," I said. "Do you know what he's capable of? Or even what he's already written about my dad?"

My father frowned and said, "Jasmine." His tone alone told me we were done, that he was right, and I had no business questioning his authority. On most matters, my dad was oblivious and I could get away with anything. Business-related stuff was the only exception.

"Fine," I mumbled. Before I headed upstairs, I went back to my dad's office and picked up the phone, still hoping I could reach Charlie. His phone went right to voice mail and I left a message.

"Charlie, it's me. Jasmine. I know you don't want to talk to me, but please listen. You can't go to Australia. I need your help. It's about Austin's screenplay. It's not Austin's. I mean, it was his copy, but he didn't write it. I did. And I didn't make the story up. I changed everyone's name, but basically, it's the story of my life. I wrote about us, Charlie. If you read it, if you saw what was in it, you'd understand why I had to end things between us and I hope it makes sense to you. I hope you don't hate me, but I'm not calling to apologize again. There's a lot of stuff in the story that can't get out. I need to stop this, somehow, and I need your help. I think if you talk to your parents, you can get them to pull the plug. Or if it's too late, you can at least warn them. They deserve to know the truth, Charlie. So please, please, please call me back. And while I'm asking for the unlikely, please don't leave. Or at least, don't leave tomorrow."

I hung up the phone and sank down into my dad's chair, feeling better than I had all night. It was a relief, finally telling someone the truth. Even if that someone was actually just voice mail. Charlie would get the message and he'd understand. He had to call me back. And he'd have to help.

I placed my cell phone next to the phone on my dad's desk and tried to will at least one of them to ring.

My dad's phone did just a few moments later. I picked it up, giddy over hearing the sound of Charlie's real, live voice at the other end of the line. "I'm so glad you called back," I cried.

"Jasmine," he said. "Please don't call me anymore."

"Aren't you going to help?" I asked.

"Help you with what?" asked Charlie.

I couldn't bring myself to rattle off all the gory details again. "With everything I mentioned in my message."

"I didn't listen to it."

"Well, you should," I said. "You have to. It's about the—"

"I don't *have* to do anything, Jasmine. I erased your message."

"But—"

"Please stop calling. Please just leave me alone. You've already done enough damage."

"Wait, you can't . . ."

I stopped talking because it's not like I could reason with the dial tone. I placed the phone back on its cradle, stunned. I can't believe Charlie hung up on me. I can't believe he erased the message without listening to it.

I can't believe I am in this mess alone.

Trudging up the stairs, I could still hear Dad and GiGi fighting.

Bits of their conversation drifted up, invading my bedroom, even though my door was closed and my head was buried under my pillow.

Dad: "I told you when we got married that I wanted nothing to do with your career."

GiGi: "If you loved me, you'd do everything you can to help."

Dad: "Some people are harder to help than others."

GiGi: "What's that supposed to mean? Are you saying I can't act?"

Dad: "I don't need to say it. Your performances speak for themselves."

Yikes, that was cruel.

True, but cruel.

Soon, the front door slammed with a powerful boom that echoed through the house.

Then there was silence.

CHAPTER SIXTEEN

WHEN I WENT DOWNSTAIRS THE NEXT MORNING, I was pleasantly surprised to find the kitchen both fruit smoothie and GiGi free. Dad and Jett sat hunched over their bowls of Lucky Charms. A large pot of coffee brewed on the counter. Everything was peaceful, back to normal.

(What I call "normal" are the quiet moments when Dad is in between wives, and it's just the three of us at home. Duke tells me I should more accurately define these brief stints in time as "wishful thinking," but whatever.)

"Morning." I was careful to acknowledge that it was morning, without committing to whether it would be a good one or not. After all, GiGi could still flit into the kitchen in her pink silky bathrobe.

Dad and Jett both grunted.

After pouring myself some coffee, I joined them at the table and asked, "Is GiGi still sleeping?"

"She's not here," my dad said.

Jett looked up from his cereal. "Where is she?"

Dad shrugged. "Shopping, probably. Or maybe at the gym."

I'm surprised he couldn't come up with a better lie. It wasn't even nine o'clock yet. No stores were open. And GiGi didn't *go* to the gym. The gym—or at least her personal trainer—came to her.

Still, I let it slide in the hopes that last night's screaming match meant she was out of the picture. Out of both pictures, I mean: *Cold-Blooded, Two-Timing Rat,* and my actual life. It was Thursday, December 24, and this was the best early-Christmas present I could hope for.

Because if GiGi had moved out, maybe Jett would finally figure out how messed up this entire situation was and stop seeing her. Or better yet, maybe GiGi would choose to wash her hands of our entire family. Either way, it would solve a major problem.

Then, all I'd have to stress over was the movie coming out. And that was an entire year away, which left me plenty of time to figure out how to explain it. Maybe I could even pull a Charlie and move to Australia. He wasn't the only one who could study abroad. I made a mental note to talk to my guidance counselor as soon as I got back to school.

As my dad brought his bowl to the sink, he said, "So, about Ixtapa. I know we're supposed to leave tomorrow, and I'm sorry to spring this on you now, but there's a slight chance that I'll be too crazy with work, so we may have to cancel."

Sure, Dad, I thought. *It's work and not your personal life that's crazy.* Still, if this meant GiGi was gone for good, I was more than happy to sacrifice a vacation. "That's fine," I said. "I don't really care."

"But pack, just in case," Dad continued.

"Is this about last night's fight?" I couldn't help but ask.

"What fight?" Jett and my dad asked at the same time.

"About the roll of Jess, in *Cold-Blooded.*" I was surprised that my dad had to be reminded. Or maybe he was just pretending to be clueless. Either way, I was determined to show my support. "It was so manipulative of GiGi to make that announcement in front of everyone. I'm so glad you didn't fall for it, Dad. Because I've read the script and the part isn't right for her at all. Jess is edgy. She's smart. At the very least, she's a brunette. That's not exactly something GiGi could pull off. Now, maybe if EggBrite was doing another *Snakes on a Plane* rip-off and needed a pretty victim with an earsplitting scream . . ."

Dad glared at me, clearly annoyed. I'd gone too far. I knew I'd gone too far, but I couldn't help myself.

"That's not the problem," he said. "Under normal circumstances I wouldn't mind leaning on the director to use GiGi, but as it turns out, there's a more bankable star interested in taking the role. I can't just hand it to GiGi because she's my wife."

"Who's interested?" I asked. "Because I have some ideas. I was thinking Natalie Portman or Alexis Bledel. They may be too expensive, but even if you just get their type, I think the strength of the writing alone will carry this film. You don't need a big-name star. In fact, this movie could probably serve as a breakout role for a lesser-known actress."

"Actually, Paris Hilton is interested," Dad replied. "Which would be a major coup for us."

I laughed. "Very funny. Okay, seriously. Who are you thinking of?"

"I am serious. I know she's fallen out of fashion, but that just means she's ready for a comeback."

Jett looked up from his cereal. "I think that's an excellent idea. Um, when can I meet her?"

This had to be a mistake. "Okay, Dad, obviously you're confused. Paris Hilton must be considering the lead in some other movie, because if she knew what this film was about, she wouldn't be into it. Jessica Brown is a complicated and serious yet fun-loving person dealing with some major family drama. I'll explain it over dim sum. Do you want to go today? And should I pick you up at your office, or would you rather meet at Empress Pavilion? It's all the same to me."

"Dim sum?" My dad gave me a blank look.

"We had plans to discuss Austin's screenplay over dim sum, remember? I hope you're still free, because I have some ideas about set design and the music score as well."

"Oh, right. Well, before you tell me what you're thinking, you should probably read the new version," said my dad.

"New version?" I asked.

He nodded. "There have been some changes. No offense to Austin. It was an impressive effort for a college kid, but he's not an experienced writer."

"Wait, what are you saying?"

Dad shrugged. "Only that the story needed some tweaking. They always do. You know that."

"Tweaking?" I asked. "They tweaked Austin's work?"

"They kept the spirit of the story and the characters intact. We have writers working around the clock. In fact, they just had the new opening scenes messengered to me this morning." Dad pulled a stack of pages from his briefcase and dropped it on the table. "Here you go."

"But don't you want to read the original version?" I asked. "It's really strong, I think. And you never even looked at it."

Wait. What's wrong with me? What was I saying? I didn't want my dad to see the original. Rewrites were good. The more tweaking the better. "Or we can just meet up and, um, talk or something."

Dad shook his head. "There's really no point, and I can't take the time. But if you finish this new material by the end of the day, maybe we can have lunch tomorrow."

"Tomorrow is Christmas," I reminded him.

"Oh, right," said Dad. "Well, we'll discuss it on the plane. Or in Ixtapa. Or at home, if we don't go. And don't you worry about GiGi. We'll work things out."

He kissed me on the forehead, waved to Jett, and was off.

"What's wrong with you?" asked Jett, once we were alone.

I didn't answer him because I was too focused on the new opening scene.

CHAPTER SEVENTEEN

Cold-Blooded, Two-Timing Rat, Second Draft

Opening scene:

The phone is ringing as the camera pans the bedroom
of seventeen-year-old Jessica Brown. Fast asleep,
she hardly stirs. She's wearing turquoise silk
pajamas. Next to her, under the covers, is a giant
purple teddy bear.

Early morning sun streams in through the window. The
room is spotless. Top-forty music posters adorn the
walls: Usher, Britney Spears, Hilary Duff, Maroon 5, etc.

The phone stops ringing, and a minute later there's
a knock on the door. In walks Pilar, the family maid.
She's carrying a silver tray with a glass of orange
juice, a plate of scrambled eggs, and a basket of
whole wheat toast.

PILAR
Jessica? Time to wake up, Jessica.

JESS (OPENING ONLY ONE EYE)
Too early.

PILAR
Your father called from Las Vegas. He
needs to speak with you. It's very
important. He wants you to call him
back immediately.

JESS (SITTING UP)
I said it's too early! It's a Saturday
and I need to catch up on my beauty sleep.

PILAR
I'm sorry, Jessica, but your father
insisted.

Pilar sets the breakfast tray down on Jess's bed.

JESS
Is that whole wheat toast? What did I
tell you yesterday? I've switched to
seven-grain.

PILAR
Whole Foods was out of seven-grain.

JESS
Then go to Trader Joe's!

PILAR
I'm sorry.

Pilar leaves. Jess chews on the toast, with a sour expression on her face. Eventually she picks up the phone and calls her dad.

(V.O.) MAX
Good morning, Jessica honey. How did you sleep?

JESS
Just fine, until you told the maid to wake me up.

MAX
Please don't blame Pilar. She's a wonderful maid, and she's been with us for six months. You know none of them has ever lasted that long. Let's try to keep her.

JESS
I'm perfectly nice to Pilar.

MAX
Of course you are. That's not why I'm calling. I wanted to speak with you before you turned on the television. Now, you know that Ginger and I have been together for three years, and that we love each other very much. And we both love you. This doesn't mean I don't still love your mother, rest her soul. But we have to move forward with our lives. It's what she'd want.

                              JESS
         What are you saying, Dad? I don't have
         all day.

                              MAX
         Ginger and I got engaged last night.
         It's all over the news, but I knew it
         was important for you to hear it from
         me. We're planning a—

Jess hurls the phone across her room. It hits the
wall and smashes into pieces. She yanks off the
covers. Her breakfast crashes to the floor. She
marches to her closet and flings open the door.

The closet is just what every young girl dreams
about. Jess has fifty Juicy Couture outfits, one in
every color. Stacks of designer jeans: Diesel, 7
jeans, Hudson Jeans, Miss Sixty, Joe's Jeans, Yanuk.
A wall of expensive purses: Fendi, Ferragamo, Gucci,
Dolce & Gabbana, Prada. A shoe collection to rival
Mariah Carey's: Manolo Blahniks, Jimmy Choos, etc.

Just then, Jess's brother, Jake, runs into her room, happy
and excited. He holds up the newspaper so Jess can see.

The headline reads:

**STUDIO CHIEF MAX BROWN PLANS FOR A NEW LEAD IN HIS LIFE.
HE AND ACTRESS GINGER BELL ARE ENGAGED.**

                              JAKE
         Jess? Great news about Dad and Ginger.
         I'm so excited for them!

CHAPTER EIGHTEEN

THE SCENE ENDED ABRUPTLY. I WAS SO SHOCKED, so not believing this actually existed, I wanted to read it again. But first I had to get through the page of notes attached. It listed other change requests.

We're repackaging this as a PG movie, so no opposite-sex sleepovers and absolutely no allusion sex. Make Alex and Chad best friends rather than brothers. Think about turning Alex into a hip-hop DJ so we can do cross-promotions with KISS FM. Along those same lines, give Chad an after-school job at the Genius Bar in The Grove. Maybe we can get Apple to pay for product placement.

Jake needs to be smart and clean-cut, a responsible college student, who serves as a positive role model for his shallow, fashion-obsessed, lying-and-cheating sister.

The affair between Jake and his stepmother is too creepy. This won't play well in the Bible Belt, or anywhere else, for that matter, so lose any reference to it.

Same with Luke. Having a gay character

with an untraditional role in a commercial
chick flick is problematic. And Internet-
stalking? That's too much of a liability.
Cut Luke and his entire subplot.
    Most important, make Max more sympathetic.
No father would ever be that self-absorbed.

Cold-Blooded, Two-Timing Rat was completely unrecognizable.
They'd ruined my movie.

"How's the new version?" asked Jett, looking over my shoulder.

There was only one word for it. "Shocking."

For some reason, this made him laugh. "That good?" he
asked.

"This isn't a joke, Jett. It's awful. It's, what's worse than awful?
Atrocious. Embarrassing. They trashed my original. Austin's original, I mean."

"And you're surprised?" asked Jett as he leaned over and
grabbed a banana from the fruit bowl at the center of the
table.

"Aren't you?"

Jett shrugged as he peeled. "Of course not. Why would I
be when EggBrite churns out tons of bad movies every year? I
mean, what did you expect?"

"I don't know. I just thought . . ." What had I been thinking?
Nothing I could admit to.

Jett laughed. "Don't worry about it, okay? Austin wouldn't
have cared. It's just cool that his screenplay went for over a million bucks. He'd have loved that. I just wish it could've happened
when he was still alive, because then he could've told his dad to
screw himself."

I watched as Jett polished off the banana in three large bites.
"You think it's his dad's fault, what happened?" I asked.

"It's not anyone's fault."

Jett was lucky he could believe this.

"Actually, that's not true. It's my fault because I was with Austin that night he died."

"You weren't at Club Moomba." Jett glanced at me, questioning. "Were you?"

"No. I mean we were together before. Earlier that night we were hooking up and he'd wanted to stay over, but I wasn't into it." It felt weird saying this out loud. I hadn't admitted the truth to anyone, even though I've been thinking about it almost every day for the past two months. "So basically, if I'd let him spend the night, then he wouldn't have OD'd."

"Bullshit," said Jett. "You don't know that."

"Sure I do."

"Do you honestly think you could have stopped it?"

The way Jett looked at me, like I was the dumb one, it was weird. Because it reminded me of the way I usually looked at him. And I didn't like it.

"Well, obviously—"

"Come on, Jasmine. You have to know it's not that simple. If you'd let Austin stay, he probably would have dropped X the next night, or the night after that, or the night after that. Maybe all three nights in a row. His drinking was out of control too. We partied a lot in high school, but Austin got so hardcore in college, sometimes I didn't recognize him. Especially near the end. Last summer was messed up. He changed. It was like . . . like he gave up, or something."

Jett was totally missing my point. "It's not like his death was inevitable," I said. "People party like him all the time and nothing bad ever happens. Nothing this bad. If I'd let him stay . . ."

"Look, I know what you're going through. It's messed up, what happened, but there are a million 'ifs' involved, and I'm sure everyone in his life feels like that. If his dad had been less of a dickhead, if someone from the band had stood up to him, if I'd told him he was out of control. And, okay, if he hadn't partied so hard that night—maybe that's true. But who knows? You can't know. No one can."

"If he hadn't *been* there that night. If I'd let him stay . . ."

"No, listen to me. It was just awful luck, you know?" Jett's voice cracked. He pressed the palms of his hands into his eyes. "It's just fucked up, but it's no one's fault."

I'd never seen my brother cry. Not that I could see him at the moment, exactly, but I knew he was, which made my eyes tear up.

"I'm sorry," I said.

Sucking his breath in through his teeth, he shook his head. "We all are," he whispered before standing up and leaving the kitchen.

I headed upstairs to my room. Collapsing onto my bed, I buried my face in my pillow and cried.

This time, it wasn't all about Austin. I was angry and confused about the mess of my life. And mad at my brother, too. That Jett could have these moments of understanding—these flashes of being cool—and yet still act like a jerk most of the time. He'd totally betrayed our father and he had no remorse. If he hadn't gone after GiGi, or succumbed to her flirtations, or who knows how it all started—just thinking about it makes me sick—then we wouldn't be in this mess.

And what was up with the new writers? Jess wasn't the lying, cheating one.

Okay, maybe she was. But she wasn't the *only* one. It wasn't completely her fault. She was just unfortunate enough to follow in her father's and brother's tainted footsteps.

And what was up with her closet? How could they turn Jess

into a shallow and label-obsessed spoiled brat? It was insulting the way they'd twisted her character into someone who wasn't me, or even anyone I knew.

Looking around my non-pink room, which wasn't decorated with pop music posters, or next to a gigantic closet bursting with designer clothes, something occurred to me. Although EggBrite butchered my work and crushed my creative integrity by so drastically changing my words and story, in a sense they also did me a huge favor. The rewrites were completely warped and twisted. There was no way my dad would recognize himself in the story. He wasn't even there anymore. No one was. Paris Hilton could play Jess, for all I cared, because *their* Jess wasn't *my* Jess. They didn't even hail from the same planet.

They'd also cut out Duke's character completely, which meant I didn't have to worry about him getting thrown out of school.

I sat up and sniffed. Reaching for a tissue, I blew my nose. Then I splashed cold water on my face, finally understanding that this was the best thing that could have happened.

I was off the hook—completely home free.

Reaching for my phone, I called Duke so I could tell him the good news. Or, I should say, all the news. Luckily he picked up on the second ring.

"Hey, it's me," I said.

"Who?" he asked. "I don't know any me."

"Come on, Duke. I'm really, really sorry I haven't returned your calls. And that I left your house so suddenly on Monday. And I'm sorry I invited you to the Christmas party last night, just to ignore you. It was a shitty thing to do, but I can explain everything."

I told him the whole story. About GiGi and my brother, about writing the screenplay and giving it to Austin—how it accidentally got sold back to my dad and no one knew the truth. And finally, how I emerged from the mess unscathed because the new writers butchered the original to the point where it was an entirely different animal.

It felt good, finally being able to tell someone. It felt good to get away with it. Like getting an A on a test I forgot to study for. Or ditching an entire day of school and not getting caught.

"I can't believe you wrote about me stalking Mr. Stark!" Duke yelled, once I'd finished my verbal purge.

"It was my diary," I insisted. "I told you, I didn't write it to sell it. If I had, I never would have used your story for my subplot. It would have been way too risky. You know I'd never do that to you."

Duke went silent for a few moments. The quiet was making me nervous.

"Are you still there?" I asked, even though I could hear him breathing.

"I am," he said. "It's just, I don't buy your whole story."

"What do you mean?" I asked. "There's nothing to buy. EggBrite already did. For over a million bucks, remember?"

"There. That's exactly what I'm talking about," Duke said. "I don't think it was entirely accidental, and even if it was, you're too happy."

"I am not," I argued. "Okay, maybe I'm a little happy, but only because I'm off the hook. I mean, can you imagine what would have happened if my dad found out the truth? Or if he didn't realize, but someone else did, and the story ended up on *Access Hollywood*? It would have been catastrophic."

"No, listen. Let's be honest here for a minute. I buy that your family is screwed up, and I know that you feel outraged and whatever, but come on, Jasmine. You're totally stoked that EggBrite bought *Cold-Blooded, Two-Timing Rat*. The way you talked about the sale just now, I can tell, and I don't blame you.

It's a big deal. Even if you just wrote all about your life. And even if they're ruining it. Even if I'm the only one who knows."

"Why would I want to expose my brother's biggest secret? Why would I want to humiliate my father? Why would I want to tell the world that I cheated on my boyfriend with his brother?"

"I don't know. You tell me."

"I wouldn't," I insisted.

"Okay," said Duke. "Answer me this: If you were writing in your diary, like you claim, why did you change everyone's name? Why did you change details, making me skinny and into sports? Why did you call my story line a 'subplot' just now? People don't add subplots to their diaries."

"How should I know? I've never kept a diary before."

"That's exactly my point. You're not the diary-writing type. If you were, you'd know better."

"Well, maybe I just *became* the diary-writing type last fall and I'm still learning the rules. And what is a 'diary-writing type,' anyway?"

"For starters, a diary-writing type would never show her diary to her ex-boyfriend," said Duke.

"But I wanted Austin to see what he'd become. And to know that I wasn't the only bad guy."

"So it was propaganda."

"That's not what I meant."

"Did you ever think that maybe a part of you wanted to get caught, subconsciously? Like maybe you did this because you're angry at your dad for behaving like such an ass."

"My dad is the victim here. Why would I be angry with him?"

"Because he married a twenty-three-year-old he'd been dating for three weeks."

"That's just part of his charm. Some people collect antique

sports cars, and some people collect rare books. My dad collects ex-wives."

"You're like your father's number-one PR person. You should be on salary."

"That's a little harsh," I said.

"The truth hurts," Duke said.

"Okay, let's not go there. This is good news, so let's just leave it at that. Want to come over and celebrate? We can work on the Anti-Star Maps, if you want."

"I can't."

"Why?"

"It's Christmas Eve."

"And you're celebrating?" I only asked because last year, Sunshine boycotted Christmas, claiming that the spiritual aspects of the holiday have been destroyed by our country's gross displays of greedy consumerism. She'd made Duke volunteer with her to plant trees at a state park up in Big Sur, and they both came home with awful cases of poison ivy.

Duke said, "She's gone all out this year because her meditation group is coming over to celebrate. They're going to reclaim the holiday for what it once was."

"What was it?" I asked.

"Apparently something involving strings of organic popcorn and lots of wind instruments. You should see our place. She's been making wreaths out of recycled garbage. Except she recycled the garbage herself and now the entire house stinks. Actually, she's calling me now. I need to make the marinade for the Tofurky."

"The what?" I asked.

"Tofurky. It's tofu in the shape of a turkey."

"That sounds kind of gross," I said.

"Um, yeah," said Duke. "And your point is?"

"Never mind," I said. "Sorry. I shouldn't make fun. Have a great Christmas, okay?"

"Will do. You too. And congratulations on your secret sale. I'm sorry they messed with your artistic vision, but I'm glad you got away with it. And that I did too."

"Thanks."

"Anytime," he said. "But next time you decide to write a diary, do me a favor and keep me out of it."

"Sure thing," I said, before hanging up.

Lying on my bed, I stared up at the ceiling and thought about what Duke had said. Not about the Tofurky or Christmas New Age–style. I mean about my having ulterior motives when I started writing *Cold-Blooded, Two-Timing Rat.*

What if he was right and a small part of me had wanted to get caught? Was it more than just a coincidence that I chose the screenplay format when screenplays are all that my father ever bothers to read?

According to my dad, television and film represent the evolution of storytelling. Books are increasingly irrelevant, and if Dostoyevsky were alive today, he'd be writing for *Law & Order.* My dad doesn't even read newspapers, as he feels journalists are merely people not talented enough to hack it in the entertainment industry.

Maybe I started writing the screenplay as a diary, but somewhere along the way, my writing turned into something else. A hostile act. Revenge.

What if I showed it to Austin because a small, hidden, secret part of me wanted the truth to come out?

Because I did want things to change.

So did that mean I should come clean now? Tell my father the truth? Or convince Jett to fess up? Yes, we'd been saved from public humiliation. But that didn't make everything better.

That's what I was wondering when my cell phone rang. I looked down at the digital display and recognized the number immediately. Normally it was one I ignored because I so dreaded hearing from this guy.

Today I was feeling generous, so I picked up. "Hey there, Barry Wentworth. Merry Christmas."

"Is this Jasmine Green? I feel like I must have dialed the wrong number, because you're never happy to hear from me."

"First time for everything," I said. "So what can I do for you?"

"I just finished reading your boyfriend's screenplay. I have it right here in front of me, actually."

"I hear Paris Hilton is interested in the role of Jess. Isn't that just brilliant?" I asked.

"Seriously?" Barry paused. "That's surprising, since Jess seems so complicated. And she's not even blond."

"Sure, she is." I said.

Suddenly Barry's tone turned chilly. Sinister, even. "You could have changed my name, Jasmine. Or should I call you Jess? I've been wondering about that comment you made after the movie last night, accidentally calling the main character Jessica Green. And you seemed very upset to hear that GiGi was interested in the role. It was puzzling at the time, but now it all makes sense."

"What are you talking about?" I asked.

"If our conversations are accurate, word for word, then I'm assuming everything else is too. You and Austin's brother . . . your brother and GiGi . . ."

I could feel my heart beating faster, but I struggled to calm. He was bluffing. He couldn't actually know anything. It was just a lucky guess. He must have put all the pieces together and come up with this theory and now he was calling me to test it out, to see if it might be true, or to fish for information. I couldn't let him know he was right. "Barry, honestly, this isn't making any sense."

"Honestly? I don't believe you. And it doesn't matter what I say, because I have the tapes to prove it."

"Tapes?" My voice wavered.

I could picture Barry gloating as he explained. "As a journalist, I tape all of my conversations. I'll bet you didn't know that, did you, Jasmine?"

"Is that legal?" I asked.

"Oh, it's legal. Just like it's legal for me to write about your family scandal. This is going to be a big story. Very big."

This was tricky. I chose my words carefully, assuming that if he'd taped our conversations in the past, he was probably doing so now, too. "You can't prove anything because there's nothing to prove. So I told Austin about you and he used your real name to make his fictional screenplay seem more realistic. That's no crime."

"Perhaps," said Barry. "Or perhaps you and Austin collaborated on this story and it's all about your life. Or maybe Austin wasn't involved at all. Maybe they found a copy of your screenplay in his room and he got all the credit. That's what I intend to find out."

"Too bad there's nothing *to* find out," I said. "Why are you calling me, anyway?"

"Because I'd like to hear your side of the story. That would only be fair, right?"

I had to laugh. "The guy who got arrested for trying to scale the wall of the hospital where Brangelina's love child was born is talking to me about fair?"

Barry ignored that. "Meet me at South Street in Malibu in an hour," he said.

"What's South Street?" I asked.

"Look it up."

"You expect me to drive all the way to Malibu just to talk to you?"

"You're not exactly in a position to negotiate, here," Barry said.

He hung up, not bothering to wait for my reply.

I guess he didn't need to because he knew that he had me.

CHAPTER NINETEEN

BARRY WAS ALREADY SITTING IN A BOOTH WHEN I got to the restaurant, five minutes early. When I slid into the seat across from him, I realized he was also in the middle of eating a large Caesar salad. I shouldn't have been surprised. It's not as if he'd invited me out for a friendly lunch.

"Don't let me disturb you," I said, by way of a greeting.

"Sorry, I didn't wait," he said. "Please order whatever you want. It's on me." Barry talked with his mouth full, waving his fork, and sounding way too pleased with himself.

"I'm not hungry." I didn't bother adding that I was actually feeling too sick to eat.

"Suit yourself." Barry put down his fork and wiped his mouth with a napkin. "So let's get to it." He pulled a small tape recorder from the pocket of his sport coat, placed it on the table in front of me, and pressed play.

Soon I heard my very own voice: *Off the record, my dad gets married all the time. That was off record. It shows up, I'm calling your boss. No, I'm having our lawyer call your boss.*

Next I heard Barry's voice. *I don't need a sixteen-year-old telling me how to do my job. I know what off the record means.*

Then mine, again. *I'm seventeen now. . . .*

It was scary, hearing our conversation from last fall repeated back to me. Embarrassing, too. It hadn't felt that way before. Writing it, I'd been in control. Yet now my words were being used against me.

Without even thinking I reached for the tape recorder, but Barry was faster. He swept it up, popped out the tape, and offered it to me. "Be my guest. I have plenty of copies at home." His voice was taunting, daring me to take it.

I shook my head. I didn't want his stupid tape. "So you recorded our conversations. Big deal." I hoped I sounded more relaxed than I felt.

Barry grinned at me, then took another bite of his salad. I watched him chew, resenting that he was keeping me in suspense like this. He had a small piece of lettuce stuck in his beard. I didn't say anything.

Swallowing, he finally said, "The words are verbatim in the screenplay. Funny coincidence, huh?"

On the drive over here I'd come up with an explanation for that. "So Austin used actual conversations from my life in his story." I gave him my best attempt at a casual shrug. "Big deal. All that proves is that I helped him a little bit. He came to me and asked for help. He wanted his story to sound authentic, so I gave him a little bit of dialogue. Everything else is made up."

He speared a piece of lettuce.

"Look," I continued, "I understand why you'd want your little made-up theory to be true. If Austin's screenplay were based on real events and there were an equivalent to the Pulitzer Prize in your seedy tabloid world, I'm sure you'd win. But all you're doing is making stuff up. There's no way to verify your suspicions, because they're all based on lies."

Barry chewed slowly, staring at me in this way that made me feel as if I were digging my own grave. "What if I tell you I don't believe you?" he asked finally. "What if I tell you I already figured out that some of the details match up? Sure, you've changed everyone's name, but just barely: Austin to Alex, Charlie to Chad, Jett to Jake, GiGi to Ginger, and your father to Max. It's so obvious."

"Look, I told you, this was Austin's thing. And he was Jett's best friend and my ex-boyfriend, so it makes sense that we'd know all the same people. This won't be a surprise to anyone."

"I've talked to Dr. Cooper as well," said Barry. "He told me he found just one copy of the screenplay in Austin's room. No one's name was on it, so he just assumed it belonged to his son. And yet, he couldn't find the files on Austin's computer, which I find suspicious. Don't you?"

"Not really," I said, unintentionally squirming in my seat.

"Did you know that the screenplay was written using professional software? The program is called Final Draft. Maybe you've heard of it?"

I shook my head no, but Barry kept on talking.

"Well, did you know this? After someone downloads Final Draft, they have to register with the company by name, and the company keeps this information in a database. I have a source there who confirmed that Austin Cooper never registered. No one in his family did."

"Maybe he used his roommate's program." As I said this, I wondered if Barry already knew that Austin had lived alone. "Or maybe it was one of his friends', or his girlfriend Violet's program. She's a film major, you know." I hoped I didn't sound as desperate as I felt.

"Perhaps," said Barry. "But how do you explain that you bought the program, downloaded it, and registered for it last fall? This all happened right around the time we had the conversation about your dad's and GiGi's elopement in Vegas."

"Okay, you've got me." I held up my hands in surrender. "I'm guilty. I did buy the Final Draft software because I wanted to write a screenplay. I'm a big cliché, like everyone else in this town. But I didn't make it very far. Writing is really hard. Boring, too. I quit after, like, three pages. No way could I have written anything like *Cold-Blooded, Two-Timing Rat*. It's all Austin's."

"And yet, all evidence says the screenplay came from somewhere else," said Barry.

"You think someone else wrote this and then didn't come forward?" I laughed. "It went for over a million dollars. What kind of person would just walk away from that?"

Turns out, this was the wrong question to ask. Barry had many reasons. He ticked them off on the fingers of his right hand. "Someone who didn't need the money, someone who didn't want the world to know her deepest, darkest secrets. Someone who didn't want to scandalize her whole family."

Clearly, Barry was smarter than I'd given him credit for. I couldn't believe this was happening now, when I'd been so close to getting away with it. I tried to keep calm, telling myself that he couldn't actually know anything for sure. He was probably trying to scare me into confessing something, and I wasn't about to fall for it. I needed water, but when I reached for the glass, I realized my hand was trembling. I pulled it away, not wanting him to see that I was crawling out of my skin with nervousness.

But I was too late. He noticed.

"You have quite the imagination," I said, anyway.

Barry shook his head. "You can deny it all you want. But this is going to get out and it's going to be a big story."

"Nothing will get out because there's nothing to get out."

He smiled. "It's okay. I didn't expect you to tell me the truth. I don't need you to, actually, because I already have enough information without you."

I fiddled with the fork and knife in front of me. "Is this all some crazy type of revenge, for the way I've been treating you?"

"How have you been treating me?" Barry asked. "I thought we were friends."

I smirked at him.

"Don't take it personally, Jasmine. I'm just doing my job." Barry signaled to the waitress for his check.

"It's all speculation."

"Speculation backed by convincing evidence is all I need," Barry replied. "It'll make a great story."

"Whatever." I couldn't listen to him anymore. I got up and said, "I don't have time for this."

"Merry Christmas," Barry called.

As I walked away from the table, I almost collided with the waitress. I didn't turn around to see if he noticed because I sensed that he did. Well, so what. That didn't prove anything other than the fact that I was clumsy.

On my drive home I tried to convince myself that things were not as bad as they appeared. Last night's fight had sounded bad, and now GiGi was nowhere to be found.

I could only assume that her marriage with my dad was over. It *had* been four months, after all. As far as his relationships went, that's hardly a below-average time span. When the truth came out, it would be bad. Yet Dad wouldn't be quite so embarrassed because he could tell anyone who asked that he'd wised up on his own. Gossip about the past is much less incendiary than gossip about the present. And, sure, my family was in the public eye, but we weren't nearly as famous as a lot of people in this town. Maybe there would be a bigger scandal for the media to focus on: a new sex tape, or some petty theft caught on a security camera, another higher-profile celebrity marriage breakup . . . Was it too much to hope for?

By the time I got home, I'd convinced myself that things weren't really so terrible. But then I noticed GiGi's bright yellow Mercedes convertible parked in the driveway. I hoped she was just stopping by to pick up the rest of her stuff. The tanning bed wouldn't fit in her car, but her little weights certainly would. I'd be happy to pitch in and rent a U-Haul to cart away her shoe collection . . . anything to get rid of her.

Noticing my dad's car as well, I wondered if I was about to walk into the middle of a screaming match. Or maybe they were busy dividing up their stuff. My dad's lawyer makes him bring a prenup on all of his first dates for just this reason.

Inside, everything was calm. My dad was sitting in the living room, talking on his cell phone.

When he hung up, I asked, "What are you doing home? It's only three o'clock."

"We have an early flight in the morning and I need to pack," he said.

"Pack?" I asked.

"For Ixtapa," he said.

"Oh, I didn't think we were going. I saw GiGi's car out front. Is she here picking up her stuff?"

"Did someone call my name?" asked GiGi, sailing into the room. She was wearing a sombrero. Yes, a sombrero. All smiles, she walked over and gave me a hug. "I'm so excited for our first family vacation!"

"You guys are . . ." I looked back and forth between them. They seemed happy, or at least content. This was awful. "Everything is okay?" I asked.

"Never better," GiGi replied as she wrapped her arms around my dad's waist and kissed him on the cheek.

Both of them were beaming.

I'd thought listening to them fight was bad. Seeing them

now, oblivious and blissful, with no idea of what was about to happen . . . I couldn't handle it.

"I'd better get my stuff," I mumbled as I headed toward the staircase, happy to have any excuse to get away from them.

In truth, I wasn't going to pack because we weren't going anywhere. We couldn't. If we went to Ixtapa, I just knew that by the time we got back, the story would be all over the place. The press would have a field day. Handling damage control from Mexico would be too complicated. I couldn't let that happen.

Things had gone too far, and it was time to put an end to this.

When I walked by Jett's room, I heard an old Bob Marley album blasting from his stereo. Since the door was open a crack, I walked inside to find him singing along to "Keep On Moving" as he packed. He seemed ecstatic, like he was about to leave for a vacation with the girl of his dreams.

"Hey, Jett?" I yelled over the music.

He turned around, tossed a white, button-down, linen shirt into his suitcase, and smiled at me. "What's up?" he asked.

I sighed. This was worse than I'd thought.

Walking over to the stereo, I turned it off. "We need to talk," I said. "Are you and GiGi still having that affair?"

CHAPTER TWENTY

JETT'S EXPRESSION QUICKLY CHANGED FROM SURPRISE to anger. "What are you talking about?" he asked, spitting out the words in a tone that bordered on hatred. Obviously he knew exactly what I was talking about. Otherwise, he wouldn't be so upset.

Part of me questioned what I was doing. It would be so easy to back down, to say never mind. Or to tell him I was just kidding and then flee, but it was too late for that. I had to do this.

"Don't bother trying to deny it. There's no time. I saw you kiss, ages ago, out by the pool, and ever since then, well, it's obvious, Jett. I don't know how Dad has remained so oblivious, but he's going to find out, because—"

Jett interrupted me. "Why would you even say that? How is he going to find out?"

"It's all in the screenplay. Austin never wrote it. I did. *Cold-Blooded, Two-Timing Rat* is my story. It's about all of us, actually: you and GiGi and Dad, and me and Austin and Charlie. Everyone is in it, and everything, too, which will be clear to anyone who knows us in the slightest. I've been a wreck all week. But then this morning I read the new opening scenes and I thought everything would be okay. It was so different, you know? But, somehow, Barry Wentworth got a copy of the original script. He knows the truth, or he thinks he does, and you know him: He's going to keep digging until he finds some sort of scandal he can sell to the tabloids."

Jett's face turned pale. "You can't tell Dad. We'll stop Barry. There has to be a way."

I shook my head. "Believe me, if there were another way, I'd be all over it. I don't know how Barry knows, but he does, and you know how he thrives on this crap. We have no choice but to tell Dad now, before he goes public."

Jett clasped his hands behind his neck and stared at the ceiling. "I can't believe you wrote about this. What were you thinking?"

Sparks of anger flared from somewhere deep inside me. "What was I thinking?" I yelled. "What were *you* thinking? You're the one who's hooking up with our stepmom. I saw you guys kissing just one week after you got back together with Lubna. Forgetting about Dad for a second, how could you do that to her?"

"Like you're one to talk, Jazzy. At least I didn't go blabbing about my infidelities to the world."

"Well, neither did I. This was all a mistake. Look, there's no time to argue. Barry could call the house any second. Or worse, maybe he'll show up here with that new Geraldo-wannabe and a live camera. We have to prepare for an ambush."

Jett followed me out into the hallway. "Wait. You're just going to tell Dad?" he asked.

"Someone has to. So what do you think?"

Jett shook his head. "Forget it. I can't."

"Then I have no other choice."

Before he could stop me, I headed back to my room and picked up the original version of *Cold-Blooded, Two-Timing Rat.*

Knowing I needed to do this quickly, before I lost my nerve, I ran downstairs.

My dad was on the phone in his office.

"I may be a while," he whispered as I sat down across from him.

"I'll wait." I clutched the screenplay in my lap, the pages now curled from so many readings. My knees bounced up and down, nervous energy that I couldn't control.

It was hard to believe things had come to this.

When I was little, I thought the entire world revolved around my father and his movie studio. Back then there was never anything more important than his next film. Each premiere party felt like an earth-shattering event, more significant than any war or famine, earthquake or flood.

As I got a little older, and with a little help from Carmen, I was able to put things in perspective, but his passion for his job continued to be something I admired. He loved film more than anything. It was all he talked about, but I was always proud, figuring his intense, one-track mind explained why he was so good at what he did.

Yet now I'd written a movie that would ruin his reputation. And I couldn't even warn him because he wouldn't get off the phone.

"Please," I whispered. "This is important."

He shook his head and turned away. "I told you we should have gone with Letterman instead of Leno," my dad said. "We need a more sophisticated audience for this film. And what did I tell you about the trailer? It needs to be recut. Add another two seconds of Mirabella on the horse. The bouncy one, and make sure her chest is in the shot."

Dad was talking about the commercial for *The Wizard, Romeo*. The movie opened tomorrow, and he was counting on it being number one at the box office.

In the past, whether or not EggBrite's holiday movie did well always determined how much fun our Christmas would be. Three years ago his movie made so much money, he went out and bought Jett a new Hummer and me a huge gift certificate to Barneys. (And, okay, I'm not that into clothes or anything, but it was the thought that counts, right?)

The year after that, EggBrite's Christmas movie bombed. We were on vacation in St. Bart's and my dad wouldn't leave his hotel room for the entire week. Not even after Jett fell asleep in the sun and got a second-degree burn. I had to take him to the emergency room myself. At the time, it didn't phase either of us. We just accepted that Dad's moods were dependant on the status of his movies. Each month it's a different story, yet always the same in that it's tied to a box office number. It just now occurred to me that maybe this wasn't normal. And even if it was, that didn't make it right or good.

"I really need to talk to you," I whispered.

"Sorry." My dad shrugged, irritated and figuring I should know better.

The sad thing was, I did know better. As soon as I'd learned to talk, I'd learned to keep quiet when he was on the phone. Work came first, and I'd never questioned that before. No one had.

Leaning over his desk, I hung up the phone for him.

"This is important," I said.

"Jasmine!" He seemed more surprised than angry. Although it didn't really matter because, either way, I wasn't backing down.

I threw the screenplay onto his desk. "We need to talk about this."

"What?" he asked, picking it up, confused. "Is this about Paris Hilton? Because I don't understand your hostility toward her. She's a lovely young woman. Smart, too. Just very misunderstood."

"I don't care about Paris Hilton, Dad. This is about the original script. Austin didn't write *Cold-Blooded, Two-Timing Rat.* I did. And it's not exactly fiction." Since I finally had his undivided attention, I launched into the story.

When I finished, my dad just shook his head, asking, "What are you saying, exactly?"

I took a deep breath and told him the worst of it. "It's the story of the daughter of a Hollywood producer, who's having an affair with her boyfriend's brother. Basically, it's about all the drama of last fall, between me and Austin and Charlie. In the first scene, Jess finds out her dad got remarried to a starlet named Ginger. Those characters are you and GiGi. Toward the middle of the script, Jess learns that her brother and her step-mom are having an affair too, right under her father's nose."

Dad's face went pale. He stared at the screenplay, trying to understand and maybe not wanting to.

"But that's not our life," he said carefully.

"I'm sorry, Dad, but it is. There's something going on with Jett and GiGi. I saw them and I wrote about it and I didn't mean for it to get out, but it did, and—"

Grabbing the screenplay off his desk, Dad shot up and stormed past me, yelling for my brother.

"I never meant for anyone to read it!" I called. "And I'm really, really sorry."

I don't think he heard me, and I guess it didn't matter, because it was too late. He was gone.

Alone in his office, I was surprised by how calm I felt. The truth was out. Duke knew. Jett knew. My dad knew. GiGi would soon find out. And, Charlie, well, he didn't care.

The worst was over.

Moments later, I heard shouting from the living room, everyone screaming at once, so it was hard to tell who was saying what.

I headed toward the chaos, stopping just around the corner so I could watch the scene unfold without anyone noticing me.

GiGi cried, "I didn't mean to hurt you, Marvin. I don't know what came over us."

Dad said, "Jett is a child. You should be arrested."

Then Jett. "I'm twenty-one, and GiGi is twenty-three. You're the one who should be arrested."

My dad turned to him, shouting, "Well, that doesn't change the fact that I'm your father. What the hell were you thinking?"

"Don't blame Jett," said GiGi. "It's not his fault, Marvin. We rushed into things, and both of us knew it wasn't working."

"So move out," my father yelled. "Or if you had to have an affair, sleep with the pool boy or Justin Riley. Anyone but my own son."

"I knew you were jealous of Justin Riley!" GiGi shouted.

"I was being facetious!" yelled my dad.

"Well, you don't have to swear!" cried GiGi.

I couldn't take it anymore. I ran upstairs to my room and closed the door behind me, turning up the volume on my stereo to block out their voices.

Moments later the front door slammed. I ran to the window and looked out. Jett and GiGi were talking in the driveway and they both seemed pretty worked up. I wanted to yell for Jett, to tell him to come back inside and to apologize, but I was too ashamed to show my face.

Eventually, they drove away, leaving in separate cars. Not that this was any comfort, because obviously they were just going to meet up somewhere else so they could be together.

It was amazing, the mess I'd managed to create. And this was only the beginning. This was just personal. Soon the whole world would know.

I ran downstairs, stopping halfway when I saw my dad in the entryway. He was standing there staring at the closed front door—shoulders slumped, and a look of stunned disbelief on his face.

"I'm sorry." I moved forward, wanting to help, or to at least explain.

He glanced at me for just a second, which was long enough for me to see the hurt in his eyes.

Then he turned his back on me and headed to his office, shaking his head and mumbling, "Not now, Jasmine."

The house was too silent, too empty, and too angry. I headed back upstairs, not knowing what to do with myself.

I tried calling Duke, but he didn't answer. Probably because he was busy celebrating Christmas with his mom and her friends. Part of me wanted to head over there and crash the party, but I couldn't leave my dad all alone. After all I'd done to him, I had to at least stick around.

So I did what I often did when I was most depressed. I pulled out one of my mom's old movies and put it in the DVD player. Then I crawled into bed and watched. It was a silly romantic comedy—one from so early in her career, she didn't even have the lead role. But that wasn't the point. I just liked seeing her. Even though she was a stranger to me, not much more than the characters she played.

What did I know about her, anyway? That her favorite color was red. That she used to take long walks on the beach to relax. That she missed Northern California and had wanted to retire early and raise sheep. It was all so generic. Not even my aunt Peggy, my mom's own sister, could really talk about her in a way that gave me any sense of who she was.

I fell asleep before the movie ended. All that drama had exhausted me, I guess. By the time I woke up, the screen was blank.

It was dark out, hours since the fight.

I got out of bed and headed downstairs.

My dad was in his office, sitting at his desk and staring at the screenplay.

"Did you finish reading it?" I asked.

He looked up, startled, like he'd forgotten I was still in the house. "I'm on my second reading."

"I'm sorry." I sat down across from him. "I never meant to do any damage. I just wrote it to vent."

"Why didn't you say anything when you found out?" he asked. "How come you let us all believe this was Austin's?"

"Because Dr. Cooper announced it at the memorial service, in front of two hundred people. It's not like I could interrupt. And you weren't even there."

"You could have come to me afterward. You should have. We were sitting right here when we discussed it."

This was so hard to talk about.

How could I explain that we didn't actually discuss anything? That he just talked at me, in between his phone calls, and I had no chance to tell him anything. And, yes, I didn't want to tell him the truth, but he didn't give me much of an opportunity to either.

"Well?" asked my dad.

"I hate dim sum."

"What?"

"Dim sum. It gives me a headache. You always want to go to the Empress Pavilion, and I don't even like it there. I've told you that before but you always forget."

Dad stared at me hard and unblinking. "Are you telling me that you wrote this—that you sabotaged me in print and attempted to humiliate me in public—because you don't like dim sum?"

"It wasn't like that at first. And now I don't even know anymore."

My dad placed his fingertips on the pages. "But you wrote this all accurately?"

I nodded ever so slightly. "Pretty much. I guess, toward the middle, I started to embellish. Duke isn't a natural blond, you know."

Frowning, he looked from me to the screenplay. "You made me out to be such a self-absorbed jerk."

I gulped, trying to swallow the lump in my throat. Finally I had to admit it. "I wrote what I saw."

He looked so deflated, it took all my willpower not to lie and tell him I'd exaggerated, that none of it was true and I was writing fiction. But I couldn't do that. I'd been doing that for too long. "I'm sorry, Dad. But it's all true."

"Well, this is only from your point of view. You have no idea what it's like, running a company and raising two kids."

"Neither do you because you didn't raise us," I said. "Carmen did."

"Well, I hired her."

"Do you honestly think that counts?" I asked. "In your mind, is that really good enough?"

"All I'm saying is that you're not being entirely fair. You're only seeing your side of it."

"Look," I said. "I'm not going to apologize for writing what I did, because it's the truth. But I feel terrible that the story got out. That Barry has all this dirt to use against us. Please believe that I never imagined this could happen."

"This is the worst of it, correct?" asked my father. "You haven't written others."

"This is my first. It started out as my diary."

"A diary in dialogue? With set descriptions?" Dad asked.

"Does it matter at this point?"

"I suppose not," he said.

"So what are we going to do about Barry?"

"I'm not sure yet. Let me start by getting out of the deal. I'll call the Coopers first thing tomorrow."

"Tomorrow is Christmas."

Dad looked at the phone and sighed. "Then I'll have to call them now."

"So you're not mad?" I asked.

He laughed. "You destroyed my marriage, made fun of me in print, and I'm soon to be the laughingstock of this whole town."

My eyes began to tear up, yet again. "It was all an accident. I swear. I'm sorry."

"Oh, relax," he said as he picked up the phone and dialed. "We'll get through this."

CHAPTER TWENTY-ONE

DR. COOPER DIDN'T TAKE THE NEWS SO WELL. Actually, he wasn't willing to take it at all. Convinced my dad was lying, and that this was some scam EggBrite was pulling to get out of paying him for Austin's work, he threatened to sue. This set off a screaming match that I could hear all the way from the living room. The next morning, Christmas morning, Dr. Cooper's lawyer called.

Sadly, that was the most exciting thing that happened all day. Since we were supposed to be out of town, no one had bothered to pick out a tree or decorate. Not that we ever do, but this was the first year I'd ever cared. We were not a normal family, but since we were stuck in town, we could have at least pretended. I would have even settled for one of Duke's mom's smelly, recycled wreaths. At least then we'd have had something to talk about. As it was, Dad and I sat around the living room in silence, consciously not speaking about anything important.

Our Christmas dinner consisted of cereal and leftover cheese puffs from Wednesday's party. We avoided the television, both of us scared we'd see our family scandal discussed on one of those awful entertainment shows. At least the phone didn't ring. This meant Barry hadn't yet published his story. But the anticipation, the not knowing when he was going to, or even where, left us both feeling uneasy.

That night, Dad sat glued to his laptop so he could check the box office numbers of *The Wizard, Romeo* every few minutes.

After I finished reading *The Scarlet Letter* for school, I pulled out Jett's old *Fiske Guide to Colleges* and I flipped to the description of UC Berkeley. I imagined living on some campus far away from L.A. Someplace with a completely different landscape: old, brick buildings, leafy trees, and college students who were interested in philosophy and politics. I had faith that somewhere in the world there were people who didn't care about where Jessica Simpson got her legs waxed or whether or not Katie Holmes has been brainwashed. And if such a place did exist, I was intent on finding it.

"Damn it," my father yelled suddenly.

I looked up and saw that he was still focused on his computer. I panicked, thinking he'd read something about us on some entertainment news website. "What is it?" I asked.

"*The Wizard, Romeo* just slid into third place. I don't believe this shit. After all we've spent on advertising. This should have been a no-brainer."

"Maybe people don't want to watch another hackneyed twist on *Romeo and Juliet*," I said.

Dad glared at me. "Fantasy is still big, and Shakespeare never goes out of style. The *Harry Potters* were money in the bank, and so was every other *Romeo and Juliet* remake. There's no explaining this. Except that people don't know what's good for them."

I laughed, thinking he was joking. "Come on, Dad. You know the movie is lousy, right?"

"Everyone loved it at the party," he argued.

"They had to act that way. They were your guests, and half of them work for you."

Frowning, Dad turned back to his computer screen. "You really didn't like it?"

"Of course not. It's a terrible movie. Jett thinks so too, but we'd never admit that. You know how you get about your work."

Shaking his head, he refused to hear me. "It's not that bad," he insisted stubbornly.

"It stinks."

I was amazed that we were fighting about this. That he could bring himself to care about some dumb movie when his son and his wife had both left him—for each other.

How did my dad get to be this way?

There were other things that mattered, weren't there? A new movie came out every month. He changed wives almost every year. But Jett and I were probably the only kids he'd ever have. And he couldn't even be bothered to talk to us about anything other than his work.

Looking down at the college guide, I realized that if he'd been paying attention to me eleven years ago and had enrolled me in kindergarten like he was supposed to, I'd be a senior now—merely one semester away from escaping this life. Unlike Jett, when I went away to college, I actually planned on getting away. Yet now, thanks to my dad's carelessness, I was stuck here for another year and a half. It wasn't fair. Things didn't have to be like this.

And all this time I'd been feeling sorry for my father. All this guilt I'd been feeling, thinking everything was my fault. Well, maybe it wasn't, completely. If my dad didn't have such a messed-up personal life, if he hadn't married GiGi so quickly, if he'd gotten to know her better, maybe he would have realized how wrong she was for him. Maybe he wouldn't have married her, or even asked her to move in. My brother isn't exactly inno-cent here, but if they'd never had the opportunity to meet, then

I wouldn't have written about it. And none of us would be in this situation.

"What are you going to do?" I asked.

Dad shrugged. "Have an emergency meeting tomorrow and recut the trailer. Maybe buy a bigger ad in the *Times*."

"I mean about your life," I said.

He didn't even look up from the computer screen when he answered. "I'm not interested in having this conversation right now."

"Well, then, what about the screenplay?" I asked. "Could Dr. Cooper actually win the lawsuit?"

My dad shook his head. "It won't make it that far. I'll take care of it."

"How?"

"You don't need to worry about this."

"Actually, I do, because it's my life too."

Dad seemed surprised, but at least I'd gotten him to tear his eyes away from his computer screen for more than two seconds. He even set his laptop down on the coffee table and looked at me. That was a first. "I'll call a meeting tomorrow and tell my colleagues that there was a big mistake. That Austin Cooper had nothing to do with *Cold-Blooded, Two-Timing Rat*. I'll say the real writer came to me, directly, with definitive proof that he wrote the screenplay. And that we have no idea how Dr. Cooper ever got himself attached to the project."

"That's it?" I asked.

Dad nodded. "It's not going to be hard to get rid of him. Ron can't prove that Austin had anything to do with *Cold-Blooded*."

"But that still doesn't fix the Barry situation."

"I haven't figured that part out just yet."

I thought about this for a few moments. It made sense, but there were still a few things I didn't get. "Why are you making me a he?"

"Because that way it'll be harder to trace the story back to you. And to us."

"Maybe they'll think Jett wrote it. And, anyway, won't they want to meet the writer? Or at least know that he or she exists? Won't they need *someone* to sign the contract?"

"Jasmine, I'm trying here. Give me a break."

"Sorry," I said.

Neither of us mentioned that GiGi and Jett might turn out to be a bigger problem.

I knew Jett was angry, but I couldn't believe he was being so reckless. Picturing him and GiGi parading around town in full range of Barry's camera lens was horrifying.

And here I was sitting around, useless. My life was on the verge of exploding, and there was nothing I could do about it.

CHAPTER TWENTY-TWO

I WOKE UP EARLY THE NEXT MORNING AND ANXIOUSLY checked the tabloids for news of Jett and GiGi's affair, or any allusion to my father's disastrous love life. There was nothing online, and the E! channel was running an all-day exposé on celebrities' babies (best dressed and fashion disasters; who had the cutest smile and the hottest nanny or manny; which ones refused to share their toys, etc.). There was no trace of anything related to my family, which was a huge relief. But I knew I couldn't let my guard down. The news could come at any moment.

When the phone rang, I jumped—scared it was Barry, or worse, some other tabloid reporter who'd gotten wind of the scandal.

But it was Carmen. "Merry Christmas!" she said.

Ha! If only . . . Still, relief flooded through me at the sound of her voice. It had been weeks since we'd last talked. "Merry Christmas to you. How's El Salvador?"

"Everything is great here. I would have called yesterday, but I was at the hospital all day. My sister had the twins. A boy and a girl—Martin and Gabriella. Born on Christmas Day. They're beautiful, Jasmine. You should see them." She sounded elated.

"That's such great news. I'm so excited for you."

"Are you okay?" Carmen asked.

"Of course," I lied. "Things couldn't be better."

"Are you sure? Because I got your messages. What's going on up there? And what are you doing at home? I thought you were going to be out of town for Christmas."

"Our trip got cancelled."

"Why?"

It didn't seem right, burdening Carmen with my family's problems. But she had asked. "It's kind of a long story. Are you sure you want to know?"

"Of course I do. What happened?"

Taking a deep breath, I launched into an explanation of the whole messy ordeal, filling Carmen in on the worst of it: my cheating on Austin with Charlie. GiGi's cheating on my dad with Jett. My writing the screenplay about it. The Coopers selling it to EggBrite. And, finally, worst of all, Barry figuring out the truth.

Carmen was quiet for a few moments, trying to process it all, I suppose.

"So," I said. "It's kind of a mess, huh?"

"Kind of," said Carmen.

"I'm sorry to dump all this on you," I said. "It's not fair. I know you moved out and it's not your job to help us anymore."

Carmen sounded hurt when she answered me. "You're my family, Jasmine. It's not about the job anymore. It hasn't been for a long time. You know that."

"Everything fell apart when you left. GiGi wouldn't have lasted a week if you'd been living with us."

"No, probably not," said Carmen. "But that's no excuse for cheating on your boyfriend. I know things weren't great with Austin at the end, but you could have handled this better. I wish you'd told me what was going on."

"I'm horrible. I realize that. There are so many things I wish I could change about last year. . . ."

"You're not horrible, Jasmine. And we don't have to discuss this right now. For the moment, I'm just trying to figure out how Barry knows so much."

"It's weird that he figured it out. I mean, I can maybe see him being suspicious, but he's so confident."

"You have been sweeping the house for bugs, right?" she asked.

I didn't understand what that had to do with anything. "The exterminator came two weeks ago, and we don't even have a problem. I mean, sometimes ants find their way into the kitchen, but only when someone cooks, which is at the most once every few months."

"I'm not talking about that type of bug," said Carmen. "I mean wiretapping. I used to bring in a private security firm every few months to sweep the house for listening devices and hidden cameras."

"Seriously?" I asked.

"Of course. I've been doing that for the past eight years. The first thing I ever found was a nanny cam in your bedroom. It was lodged in the belly of a teddy bear. I was so angry because I thought your dad and stepmom had put it in there so they could spy on me. After days of worrying about it, I finally confronted your father. It turns out that he was surprised too. The teddy bear was a birthday gift from *The National Enquirer.* They managed to sneak cameras into celebrity homes all over the city."

"The tabloid did that?" I asked.

Carmen said, "Yes. It's not just the FBI and the CIA involved in the wiretapping of phones, Jasmine. Sometimes overzealous reporters like to play James Bond. I used to find bugs in the phone system at least once a year."

"No one ever told me."

"When you were younger we kept it from you on purpose because we were afraid it would upset you too much. Your father doesn't want you and Jett turning into paranoid people. I don't blame him for that, but I told him you were old enough to know the truth. That you needed to know for your own protection. He said he agreed. Oh, I wish I'd said something myself. I arranged for the head of the housekeeping staff to keep up with the appointments every month."

"Well, GiGi fired her last week. The entire staff, actually."

Carmen sighed. "She really is terrible. Tell me, have you seen anyone suspicious lurking around the house?"

"There were over three hundred people at the Christmas party last Wednesday."

"So it's possible that Barry managed to sneak in. Or perhaps he hired someone to do his dirty work," said Carmen.

"He wouldn't have had to. GiGi invited him."

"Barry was invited?" Carmen seemed surprised. "He was there? At the house?"

"Yes, and he even stayed for the movie. I found him in Dad's office after everyone else had left."

"Then I'm calling Pedro," Carmen said.

"Who?" I said.

"You know my cousin Pedro. The tall one with the pug, and the girlfriend with the unfortunate extensions."

"Oh, from your good-bye party last summer? The guy who's allergic to shrimp?" I asked.

"Exactly. He's a detective with the L.A.P.D. now. I'm hoping he can go to your house and check things out. I'd call the regular security company, but Barry may have connections inside. Best not to get too many strangers involved, don't you think?"

"Whatever you say," I replied.

"I'll call you right back." Carmen said.

And she did, just a few minutes later, to tell me that Pedro would swing by in an hour.

"That was fast," I said.

"Well, I told him that this is an emergency," said Carmen. She gave me the number of her sister's place in El Salvador and told me to call her as soon as I knew anything.

I hung up the phone, feeling completely stunned. Knowing there could be some sort of spy equipment planted in the house, that Barry could be listening to everything I said—it was nerve-racking.

I couldn't take it, so I grabbed my cell and the screenplay and headed outside to sit by the pool. I left another message on Jett's voice mail (the fourth since he'd stormed out) and then stared at the front cover of *Cold-Blooded, Two-Timing Rat.* I didn't need to read it again because by now I'd memorized it. Instead, I just thought about the entire mess. How I'd managed to turn an already horrible situation into something a hundred times worse.

When I was younger, I used to think there was a camera following me around all the time. Not in the sense that I thought I was being tracked by tabloid reporters, which happened to be true only some of the time. I mean I actually felt like a character playing a role in someone else's movie. Like everyone around me was just acting out specific roles. So pouring my heart out in the form of a screenplay had seemed completely natural.

The format was so clean and easy too. When I started it, I told myself that if I wrote down all of the events, and what everyone said and did, then it would start to make sense. By transforming myself and everyone I knew into characters reciting lines, I could sit back and watch, figure out where I went wrong and how to make it all better.

Except that never actually worked. And it was only just now

occurring to me why. I couldn't be a passive observer in my own life. It was impossible and stupid to pretend. I'm the one who cheated on Austin with Charlie and vice versa. I'm the one who snuck around and lied and cheated. Trying to analyze it all from afar wasn't possible. Writing about my life did not remove me from it. And blaming genetics was bullshit. We studied genetics in bio last year. I know there's no such thing as an infidelity gene. I had known all along. I cheated because I chose to cheat and it was rotten and there's no excuse. It wasn't my dad's fault, and it had nothing to do with Jett. I could be different from them just by choosing to be different. It was that simple.

Before I knew it, I heard a car pull up to the house. I ran around to the front, relieved to see Pedro in the driveway ten minutes early.

"Thanks for coming over," I said as he got out of the car.

"I'm happy to help," Pedro replied.

We went inside and I took him right to my dad's office. "This is where I found Barry. He was lurking behind the desk. I guess I should have suspected. I mean, I figured he was snooping. I just had no idea he'd go this far."

"Let's not get ahead of ourselves," said Pedro. He set his brief-case down on the floor, opened it up, and pulled out a strange-looking rectangular device. It was about the size of a shoebox and it had a handle on top. Attached to one side was a wand, similar to the kind that airport security uses when they do body checks. The other side had a bunch of dials and switches. "This is an interceptor," Pedro explained. "It'll tell us if there are any listening devices in the area."

As he turned it on, the machine emitted a low, static-y sound. Pedro waved the wand over the desk, and it let out a series of slow beeps. The noise grew louder and more frequent as he moved it toward the phone.

Soon he set down the device and slipped on a pair of gloves. Picking up the phone, he unscrewed the mouthpiece. Then, using a pair of tiny tweezers, he pulled out a small, black, oval-shaped thing and held it up to the light.

"That's the bug?" I whispered.

It was no bigger than a watch battery.

"That's the bug," he said. "And you don't have to whisper. It's not on anymore."

"It's so tiny."

Pedro pulled a small plastic bag out of his briefcase and dropped it inside. Then he unplugged the phone and put it inside a larger bag. "I'll take these down to the station and call you as soon as I know anything. But before I go, let me check the rest of the phones and all of the computers, too. Just to be on the safe side."

I handed over my cell, which was clean.

Then Pedro did a quick sweep of the rest of the house, but didn't find anything else.

He left and called me an hour later to tell me the prints on the bug definitely belonged to Barry Wentworth.

"Unbelievable!" I said.

"Actually, it's fairly typical," said Pedro. "We see this all the time. Now, do you want to press charges? We definitely have enough evidence to bring him in. And he already has a long list of similar infractions. Just last month they caught him Dumpster diving outside of Brad Pitt's house. And Halle Berry took out a restraining order on him three weeks ago."

"My, he's been busy."

"No kidding. We can arrest him over this, but then it will become a matter for the public record. That means the media will find out, and Carmen tells me that you're trying to keep a low profile."

I tried to picture Barry's mug shot on the front cover of *Us*

Weekly. It was easy enough. The problem was, any story about his spying would be accompanied by larger shots and a more in-depth investigation of my dad, me, Jett, and the Coopers.

"It's tempting," I said. "But as much as I'd like to see Barry arrested, I think I need to handle things on my own."

"That's probably wise. But do give a call if I can help in any way," said Pedro. "And you can always change your mind. I'll hold on to the evidence."

"Okay, thanks," I said.

"Anytime."

As soon as I hung up, I called Barry and asked, "Hey, how's that story coming?"

"Couldn't be better," said Barry. "I have a source at EggBrite who tells me your dad is trying to bury the movie. He ordered all of the original copies to be shredded, which isn't wise because he's only raising suspicion. But even better, I just got off the phone with Violet, who confirmed that you two met at Moomba in September. She remembers all sorts of details that match up. Everything from the sticky table covered in peanut shells to you storming out of the bar in a huff."

"Hmm," I said. "Guess you've got me. Too bad you're not going to be able to print a word of it."

"And why is that?" asked Barry.

"We had a little bug problem at the house," I said. "In fact, I just got off the phone with a friend of mine at the L.A.P.D. Funniest thing—he found one planted on my dad's phone. And your fingerprints are all over it."

There was silence on the other end of the line. Beautiful, beautiful silence.

When Barry finally spoke, his tone of voice had changed completely. "Listen, Jasmine. If I ever said or did or wrote any-thing to offend you, I'm very sorry."

"Bullshit," I said.

"These accusations you're making? They're serious." He sounded worried, as he should.

"You sound kind of nervous, Barry. It's probably because of your long police record. One more infraction and you'll go to jail. Isn't that right?"

"You know that would destroy me," said Barry.

"Just like my dad will be destroyed if you print that story."

"Know what? I'm not so interested in the story behind this movie. If there even is a story, which I doubt."

"Hey, if all goes well, there won't even be a movie," I said. "So does this mean you won't be writing about me?"

"Not this week," said Barry. "And never about *Cold-Blooded, Two-Timing Rat*, I promise."

"That's not good enough," I said. "I want you to leave me alone for good. And not just me, but Dad and Jett, too."

Barry sighed. "Jasmine, I knew you were tough, but I had no idea you could be this ruthless."

"Well, honestly, I had a little help," I said.

"From who?" Barry wondered.

I smiled. "From none of your business."

After calling Carmen to tell her the good news and to thank her profusely, I called my dad at his office.

"Barry is no longer a problem," I sang into the phone.

"Really?" My dad sounded surprised.

I quickly filled him in. The fact that his phone was bugged didn't faze him too much. He was just surprised that he hadn't thought of it himself, but I guess he had a lot on his mind these days.

I asked him if he'd heard from Jett or GiGi.

He hadn't, but was confident that Jett would show up soon, since he'd just cancelled all his credit cards.

"What's going on with *Cold-Blooded*?" I asked.

"We had a meeting about it this morning."

"Were they surprised when they found out that Austin wasn't the real writer?"

"You can say that." My dad sounded distracted. His other line was ringing in the background. "Hang on a second? I need to take this."

Dad kept me on hold for a while, but for once, I didn't mind.

When he finally came back, I asked, "Was that Jett?"

"No," he said. "That was Steve Donaldson, the head lawyer at EggBrite. It seems that halting the production of *Cold-Blooded* isn't going to be so easy."

"How come? It's not like they've started shooting," I said.

"True, but we moved quickly on this. As you know, EggBrite is already paying to have the movie rewritten, and we've hired a director and some of the actors. Contracts have been signed. And it's a high-profile deal. Steve says if I don't resolve this case with the Coopers, well, things are going to get messy."

"How can Dr. Cooper even have a case when he can't prove that Austin wrote the screenplay?"

"Because he's greedy, and because I can't prove that Austin *didn't* write it. Obviously we're in no position to reveal the real writer's identity."

"Is there anything I can do?" I asked.

"No, you've done enough. I'm glad you got Barry off the case, but I can handle things from here," he said before hanging up.

The thing is, he was wrong. There was still something I could do. It was kind of a long shot, but I had to at least try.

CHAPTER TWENTY-THREE

FOR SO LONG I'D SEEN DR. COOPER AS THIS STRICT, one-dimensional guy who was constantly fighting with Austin. He'd always had so many expectations and was so insistent that Austin become someone he wasn't: a serious, science-minded guy, ambitious in the narrowest sense of the word. I tried to imagine what he was going through now.

In Dr. Cooper's mind, it was like Austin was a disappointment in his life, but in his death he'd redeemed himself by becoming something more. A writer, someone with great promise, gone before his time.

I realized that my father had been wrong about him all along. Dr. Cooper wasn't greedy or manipulative. He didn't announce the news of the deal at the memorial service to put pressure on EggBrite. He was just a sad old guy who'd lost his son. He'd made the announcement because he was proud of Austin. This image, this hope—it was all he had left. And now we were trying to take that away from him. No wonder he'd reacted so strongly.

But I couldn't go on pretending. He needed to know the truth.

I gathered all the evidence I could find—my laptop, earlier

drafts of my screenplay, some character notes I'd written during a particularly boring American history lecture—and got into my car. As I drove over to the Coopers', one thing became clear. I needed to stop lying to myself.

Maybe *Cold-Blooded, Two-Timing Rat* had started out as my diary, but it sure hadn't ended up that way.

It was too clean and easy, what I'd done. Pretending everyone in my life could be reduced down to specific roles. . . . Jett as the jerky older brother; my dad as the womanizing Hollywood executive; his wives a myriad of stick-figured clones, distinguishable only based on whether they preferred Dolce & Gabbana or Prada; Austin as the arrogant ex; and Charlie as the nice nerd.

Life was more complicated. People were more complicated. Jett wasn't all bad. My father was more than his public persona. Sure, GiGi was a disaster in stilettos, but some of my stepmoms had been cool. Austin hadn't always been a jerk, and Charlie wasn't perfect.

What I wrote was a screenplay—a story, not a diary. And there was no point in denying it. Nor was there any point in hiding it.

When Dr. Cooper answered the door, he seemed surprised to see me.

"Jasmine?" he said, blinking. "Charlie left yesterday. I thought you knew."

"I'm not here to see Charlie." Not waiting to be invited inside, I walked past him and headed into the living room. "I need to talk to you about the screenplay."

"You don't want to get involved in this mess. I'm surprised your father allowed you to see me."

"Well, actually, he doesn't know I'm here," I said as I sat down on the living room couch and opened up my book bag.

Dr. Cooper sat across from me, looking puzzled. "I don't understand."

"Austin didn't write *Cold-Blooded, Two-Timing Rat.* I did, and I'm sorry I didn't tell you before. Everything happened so quickly, and well, if you think about it, you'll see. And if not, I can prove it." I handed him the early drafts and some of my notes. Then I opened my laptop and showed him the various documents in the *Cold-Blooded* folder on my desktop.

He took it all in silently, finally asking, "If you wrote this, why didn't you come forward earlier?"

"Because it's true," I replied. "Everything I wrote about, I mean."

"Oh," said Dr. Cooper. Then, realizing the extent of it, I suppose, he said, "Oh," again. This time more pointedly.

"I gave Austin my copy, but I didn't write the screenplay because I wanted to sell it. Not at first, anyway." I realized I was implicating myself even further, but I'd already come this far. "I'm sorry for how I treated Austin. Charlie, too. I tried to apologize to him myself, but he's not really talking to me at the moment. Not that I blame him, because, well, that's a long story. Of course, you read *Cold-Blooded*, so basically you know the story."

Dr. Cooper leaned over. Resting his elbows on his knees, he stared at the floor. "You think you know your children. . . ."

"It was wrong, what I did. Cheating on Austin, falling for Charlie. I feel terrible. I never meant to hurt either of them."

"When that reporter called the other day and started asking questions, well, I started to wonder. And I suppose I should have known that Austin wasn't a writer."

"Actually, Austin was a writer, but in a different way." I handed him the Canadian Bacon CD.

Dr. Cooper stared at it, turning it over in his hands and not quite getting it. "What's this?" he asked.

"It's Austin's band. I know you weren't really interested in that part of his life, but maybe now . . . Well, you can have this copy. Austin gave it to me a while ago. He put stars by the ones that he wrote."

"He wrote that many?" Dr. Cooper traced his fingers along the list, maybe finally seeing that Austin had been more than just a disappointment. At least, I hoped he could see that.

"He did, and they're really good. And I've been thinking. That foundation you want to start? I think it's a good idea. Who knows how all this will work out, but if the screenplay sale still goes through, I think we should still use the money for scholarships in Austin's name—if you don't mind. There's just one thing: I think we should change the requirements. I think it would be more fitting—that it would be truer to Austin's memory—if we gave scholarships to students who study music."

"That's an interesting idea," he said softly.

"It's just something I've been thinking about." I got up to leave. Before I walked out the door, I turned around and said, "It was wrong, how I treated Austin. I wish I'd been a better friend to him. There's no excuse for what I did, and I'm really sorry about everything that happened."

When Dr. Cooper finally looked up at me, his eyes were glossy with tears. "You're not the only one who needs to feel sorry."

CHAPTER TWENTY-FOUR

IF MY LIFE WERE A MOVIE, THE SAGA OF THE SCREENPLAY would have a happy ending, and this would be the final scene. It would take place at the beginning of summer, on a warm evening in early June.

The camera would slowly pan the walls of my dad's office, which would be covered with framed photographs. There would be pictures of my dad with various celebrities: Kate Hudson, Angelina Jolie, Ashton Kutcher, and Johnny Depp, among others. Finally, in the center of the wall, blown up to twice the size of all the others, there would be a picture of my dad with Jett and me.

The camera would then travel through the halls and out the door, past the pool out back, and into the screening room, where me, my dad and brother, Carmen, Duke, and Lubna would be watching the rough cuts of *Cold-Blooded, Two-Timing Rat.*

This almost happened in real life. The only difference is that my original screenplay went through many rounds of rewrites. EggBrite finally settled on telling the story of a spoiled rich girl who can't handle the fact that her nanny and her father have fallen in love. EggBrite packaged it as a *Maid in Manhattan* meets *Clueless* meets *Spanglish* meets *The Wedding Planner.*

Dad was happy because they cast Alec Baldwin to play him.

Carmen was happy because they went with Salma Hayek for her role.

Jett was crushed that they cast that nerdy guy who plays Seth Cohen on *The O.C.* to play him, but everyone else thought it was hilarious.

GiGi didn't land the teenage lead. She didn't get cast as the stepmother, either. In fact, she wasn't in the movie at all, and neither was Paris Hilton.

They went with an unknown actress to play Jess. Not that it mattered, because the movie they made had nothing to do with me or my life. I don't think they kept even one line from the original screenplay, although it was hard to tell. It was so ridiculous, we laughed throughout the screening, so I missed most of the dialogue.

When it finally ended, Lubna was the first one to speak. "I can't believe I'm not in it at all," she said, in mock-outrage. "What's up with that? Pakistanis can only play terrorists or gas station attendants?"

"You didn't live here last year," I said. "And, believe me, you should consider yourself lucky to have been spared."

"That's so true," said Duke. "It's worse for me. To have been in the original version and to be cut out completely is much more insulting than to have never been in the story at all."

"Do you think it's going to do much business?" I asked. Not only was I curious, I also had a financial interest at stake. After I'd come forward as the real writer, Dad helped me renegotiate the deal with EggBrite. So now I owned a piece of the backend. (We'd all managed to save face, too. There were so many rounds of rewrites that no one at EggBrite remembered the original clearly enough to trace the characters back to my family.)

"I don't know and I don't care," said my dad, who'd left EggBrite months ago.

Okay, he got fired, but it was for the best. Ever since he left, he's been taking time to relax, have long lunches, and hang out with Jett and me.

More important, he was on a dating sabbatical. After he and GiGi filed for divorce, Jett and I sat Dad down and had a talk with him. We told him that things had gotten ridiculous. He was a grown man—middle-aged, even—and he had to start acting the part. He promised us that he wouldn't get married or ask anyone to move in with us for an entire year. After that, he could do whatever he wanted, because by then I'd be away at college.

That was my hope, anyway. First I needed to actually get in to college, and hanging out in the screening room wasn't going to help me there.

The SATs were only two weeks away and I still had some practice tests to get through. I said good night to everyone and headed upstairs to my room so I could study.

Twenty minutes later, as I sat on my bed, going over vocabulary, I noticed a dark shadow looming outside.

Someone was on my balcony, knocking on my window.

I grabbed my phone, intent on dialing 911, but something stopped me. I had this weird feeling that whoever was at my window might be someone I wanted to see.

Just to be safe, I held my cell phone in one hand and a baseball bat in the other. Approaching the window slowly, I peeked behind the shade and found Charlie Cooper standing on the other side.

My heart flipped over in my chest at the sight of him on my balcony.

And when Charlie saw me, he smiled his crooked, adorable smile and his eyes lit up.

I dropped the bat and my phone and pried open the window.

"What are you doing here?" I asked as I helped him climb in. Rather than answer me, he gave me a hug.

"I'm so sorry," he said.

"No, I'm sorry. This was all my fault. I should have been more honest with you. We never should have—"

"It's okay," Charlie whispered.

"No, it's not." I pulled away. "Things have been so crazy since you left. You have no idea what's been going on."

"Actually, I think I do." Charlie reached into his backpack, pulled out a copy of *Cold-Blooded, Two-Timing Rat*, and dropped it on my desk. It was weird, seeing the original bound pages. I got the chills just looking at them. "Where did you get that?"

"My father sent it to me a few months ago."

"Your father?" I asked. "Why?"

"I'm not sure," Charlie admitted. "But I'm glad he did, because I get it now. Why you felt so guilty, I mean. Why things were such a struggle. You never told me what was going on with Jett and GiGi. If you had, I would have understood. Or maybe I wouldn't have, back then, but I do now. I understand why you had to end things. Why you were so worried about being like her."

"I'm sorry I drove you out of the country," I said.

Charlie shook his head. "You didn't. Honestly, I wanted you to think that you did, and that it was your fault, but this wasn't about you. My brother died. It still seems weird, saying it. Worse than that, sometimes I'll forget, and then all of the sudden it'll hit me and it's so intense. Being at home was hell. Just the worst. I couldn't stand being in L.A. Everything reminded me of Austin. Last year was messed up. I needed to get away just to breathe."

"It was horrible, what we did," I said. "Dating behind his back like that."

"It was a nightmare, what happened, but it's too late to change that. And there's no rule that says we have to be over. That we can't still be friends, at the very least."

Friends. It had an interesting ring to it. But not in that mid-nineties-sitcom way.

No, actually, friends seemed right. In fact, I couldn't have written a more perfect ending. Although, luckily, I didn't need to. Pouring my heart and soul onto the page wasn't necessary anymore. If any new drama came up, I knew I had friends and family to talk to. Not to mention a standing date for power yoga with Carmen every Saturday.

Of course, technically, I never finished writing *Cold-Blooded, Two-Timing Rat.*

Maybe this was the ending I've been waiting for.

Or maybe this scene would be perfect for the sequel. . . .

CHAPTER TWENTY-FIVE

FADE IN: Interior: Jess Brown's bedroom. She's studying in her room. Suddenly she sees a dark shadow pass across her window. She goes over to investigate. Peeking behind the shade, she sees Chad.

They share a smile.

And possibly more . . .